Do you know the Monkey Man?

Do you know the Monkey Man?

Dori Hillestad Butler

PEACHTREE
ATLANTA

Published by
PEACHTREE PUBLISHERS
1700 Chattahoochee Avenue
Atlanta, Georgia 30318-2112
www.peachtree-online.com

Text © 2005, 2018 by Dori Hillestad Butler

First United States trade paperback edition published in 2018.

Jacket design by Adela Pons
Book design by Melanie McMahon Ives

Manufactured in September 2017 in United States of America by LSC Communications in Harrisonburg, VA.
10 9 8 7 6 5 (hardcover)
10 9 8 7 6 5 4 3 2 1 (paperback)
HC: 978-1-56145-340-5
PB: 978-1-68263-038-9

Library of Congress Cataloging-in-Publication Data

Butler, Dori Hillestad.
Do you know the monkey man? / written by Dori Hillestad Butler.—1st ed.
p. cm.
Summary: While searching for the father who left her and her mother ten years ago, thirteen-year-old Samantha begins to believe that the twin sister who supposedly died when they were three years old is still alive.
ISBN 978-1-56145-340-5
[1. Missing persons—Fiction. 2. Fathers—Fiction. 3. Twins—Fiction. 4. Family—Fiction.] I. Title.

PZ7.B9759Do 2005
[Fic]—dc22
                                                          2004024798

For my friend, Paula, who was there when I first started thinking about this book…at age thirteen. (See? I always told you I'd dedicate a book to you one day. And I know you always believed I'd do it.)

Acknowledgments

While the act of writing is a solitary activity, no book is ever truly written alone. I'd like to thank Doug Vance of the Coralville Police Department for talking with me about the situation described in this book and for allowing me to interrupt his day on several occasions to ask "just one more question"; Judge E. W. Hertz for patiently and thoroughly answering all my questions on family law; Mary Scarborough for putting me in touch with Mr. Hertz in the first place; my Sisters in Ink friends for letting me ramble on about this project two years in a row; my editor, Lisa Banim, for guiding me in the right direction; and all the people at Peachtree who helped make this book a reality. I'd also like to thank my wonderful husband and children, who give me time and space to write every day. . .and without whom I wouldn't be who I am today.

—DHB

Chapter 1

I'm dying here, Sam," my best friend Angela panted as we started up another hill. "Where *is* this place?"

I wasn't enjoying the long bike ride any more than Angela was. It was so hot out it felt like we were riding our bikes inside an oven. My shirt was soaked with sweat, my butt was numb, my legs were ready to fall off, and let's not even talk about my hair. But I shifted to an easier gear on my bike, wiped my sweaty forehead against my arm, and said, "It's got to be around here somewhere."

"I don't know." Angela stopped her bike. "This doesn't look right."

"The ad in the Yellow Pages said North Star Road," I said over my shoulder. "This is North Star Road." But Angela had a point. The houses were pretty spread out around here. There were no businesses anywhere in sight. North Star Road would turn into Highway 1 up ahead and when it did we wouldn't even be in Clearwater anymore. We'd be out in the country.

I glanced around, searching desperately for some clue—*any* clue—that we were headed in the right direction. There was a sign in front of an old house up ahead. Could that be the place?

"Sam!" Angela yelled as I kept pedaling. "Where are you going?"

I didn't stop until I was close enough to read the sign. The paint was peeling, but I could still make out the black-and-white drawing of a lady gazing into a crystal ball and the words "Psychic Readings by Madame Madeline."

Yes! "This is it!" I told Angela.

Angela sighed and walked her bike the rest of the way to me. She glanced over at the house behind the sign and curled her lip in disgust. "You've got to be kidding," she said.

The house did look sort of scary. Like the sign out front, it hadn't been painted in a very long time. Four rotted steps led to a rickety front porch. There was even a window boarded over upstairs.

"I don't know if this is such a great idea," Angela said slowly.

I had to admit I wasn't entirely sure myself. I mean, I'd never been to a real, live psychic before. I didn't even know for sure that Madame Madeline *was* a real psychic. Let's face it, most of them are probably fakes. But I think there are at least a few people out there who really do have some psychic abilities. People who help the police solve crimes or whatever. I had no idea whether Madame Madeline ever did anything like that, but she was the only psychic we had in Clearwater, Iowa. And well, she had four stars on Yelp.

"You don't have to come with me if you don't want to," I told Angela as I wheeled my bike over to a lamp-post.

"No, no," Angela said, trailing along behind me. "I said I'd go with you and I will. I mean, if you're sure you want to do this. I just think there has to be a better way of finding your dad than going to a psychic."

"Like what?" I asked. My mom was no help. She hated my dad. She got all bent out of shape anytime I even brought him up in conversation.

There were no relatives on his side of the family to ask. Or if there were, I'd never met them. I know my dad grew up here in Clearwater, though. I asked some of the older people in my neighborhood if they remembered him. Everybody did ("Such a shame, what happened," Mrs. Inger tsk-tsked.), but nobody seemed to have any idea where he was.

Mrs. Sandvick told me she used to play cards with my dad's mom, which proved I had a Grandma Wright out there somewhere. It also made me wonder whether I had any aunts, uncles, or cousins on my dad's side. Mrs. Sandvick couldn't remember whether my dad had any brothers and sisters, but she did remember that Eva Wright cheated at cards and she wasn't sad when Eva moved away. Then she wanted to know why I was asking so many questions. I was afraid she'd tell my mom I'd been nosing around, so I took my search elsewhere. To the Clearwater Public Library.

There's a sign by the reference desk that says if they don't know the answer to your question, they'll find it. But when I talked to a reference librarian, the woman sort of pinched her lips together and said they don't get involved in family affairs.

I tried the internet too. I searched for him on every social media site I could find. But do you have any idea how many Joseph Wrights there are in the world? Millions! I had no idea how to figure out which one was my dad.

How else was I supposed to find him when he'd totally disappeared off the face of the earth? As far as I was concerned, Madame Madeline was my only hope.

"Fine. We're here, so let's give it a shot," Angela said.

We locked our bikes to the lamppost and started up the front walk. I wished I had a comb. I had to settle for running my fingers through my hair to untangle it and pouf it up a bit. But it was so humid out, I knew it wouldn't do much good.

"Should we ring the bell or will Madame Madeline somehow sense that we're here and come to the door on her own?" Angela said, wiggling her fingers.

I rolled my eyes.

But before we even reached the first step, Madame Madeline did open the front door. Or someone did. She came out onto the porch.

Angela and I gawked. I don't know what I thought a real psychic should look like, but this woman was definitely not it. She looked...well, like a regular person. She wore a yellow sundress like the ones they sell at Walmart with matching flip-flops, and she had wavy honey blond hair that hung to her waist. She was pretty, but if you asked me, she could've used a little eye makeup or blush, something to give her face some color and hide her freckles.

"Do you girls want something?" She looked at us curiously.

I glanced at Angela, then took a step toward Madeline. "Um, we were wondering," I began. I didn't know how to talk to a psychic. Did I even have to talk, or could she read my mind?

"I mean…" I stammered. "I…uh, saw your listing on Yelp, and, well—"

"Are you Madame Madeline?" Angela blurted out. One thing about Angela, she never has any trouble saying things straight out.

The woman leaned against the cracked doorjamb. "Yes, I am. What can I do for you?"

I cleared my throat. "There's something I have to know," I said, my heart thumping. "I'd like to have a—whatever you call it—a psychic reading?"

At first Madame Madeline didn't say anything. She just inspected me from head to toe. It was kind of unnerving, if you want to know the truth.

"You really are psychic, right?" I had to ask.

She smiled. But instead of answering my question, she said, "Generally I do readings by appointment only."

Appointment? I groaned to myself. Did that mean we'd just biked all the way out here in the blazing heat for nothing?

Madame Madeline checked her watch. "But I have a few minutes. Why don't you come in?" She held the door open and a black-and-white cat nuzzled her leg.

Angela raised her eyebrow at me. I could still change my mind. But I wasn't going to. We stepped inside.

The cat meowed at us, then turned and padded up the stairs.

I have to say, the inside of the house looked a lot better than the outside. I expected it to be all dark and dreary with long strings of beads hanging in the doorways. But this place was bright and cheerful. No beads. Sunlight poured in through two tall living room windows. And everywhere you looked there were plants—on tables, bookshelves, the windowsills, and the floor.

"I usually give readings in here." Madame Madeline led the way to a small dining room, then turned to look at us. "Who wants to go first?"

"Oh, I'm not doing this." Angela shook her head and backed away. "Just her." She jabbed her thumb at me.

"Then you can have a seat over there." Madame Madeline directed Angela toward a rocker in the living room. "And you—what's your name?" she asked me.

"Sam," I answered.

"Sam? Is that short for Samantha?"

I nodded.

"Hmm," she said, her index finger tapping against her chin. "I believe that's an old Aramaic name. It means 'listener.'"

I could hear Angela snorting in the other room, but

I pretended I didn't. "I don't know," I said to Madame Madeline with a nervous smile. How did she know what my name meant when I didn't?

"Well, why don't you join me here at the table?" Madame Madeline pulled out a tall, straight-back wooden chair for me. I slowly eased myself into it and she sat down beside me.

"So, the reason I'm here—" I began.

"Shh!" She put her finger to her lips. "May I see your hand?"

I held out my hand. I figured she was going to read my palm or something, but she was more interested in the back of my hand than my palm. She traced her finger over the big vein that stuck out. It tickled a little.

I glanced over my shoulder at Angela. I could tell she was trying really hard not to laugh as she rocked back and forth. I shouldn't have asked her to come with me.

I turned back to Madame Madeline. "Don't you want to know why I'm here?" I asked, my foot tapping against my chair.

"I know why you're here," she replied. She still had hold of my hand. "You have questions. Many questions. And these questions cannot be answered through normal channels."

"Um...yeah." Something like that.

"I can't guarantee a specific answer to your questions," Madame Madeline said. "All I can do is tell you what I see. The answers to your questions may be there or they may not. Do you understand?"

I nodded.

"Do you wish to continue?"

"Sure," I said.

"Then my fee is fifty-five dollars. Payable up front, please."

"Oh." I blinked. "Okay." I reached into my front pocket, pulled out a wad of hard-earned baby-sitting money, and counted out fifty-five bucks. If Madame Madeline could tell me where my dad was, she'd be worth every penny.

Madame Madeline stuffed the bills into the pocket of her sundress, then peered into my eyes. I felt like she could see all the way to my soul.

Finally, she spoke. "You're a bright girl, Sam. You do fine in school."

"I guess that depends on your definition of 'fine,'" I mumbled. I got mostly B's in school. Sometimes I even got a C in math or gym. In my mom's book, C's were practically failing.

"And you have friends," Madame Madeline went on.

Friends? Yes. Popularity? No.

"It isn't school or your social life that brings you here today. It's something else." Madame Madeline picked up my hand again and turned it around. "It's your family. Something about your family is out of balance. Something troubles you very deeply."

"Yes!" I leaned toward her eagerly.

"Your family is divided. There are two on one side and two on the other."

I didn't quite know what she meant by that. "There are only two people in my family," I said. "Just me and my mom. Unless you count Bob. My mom and Bob are getting married pretty soon."

"Bob is your mother's fiancé?" Madame Madeline asked.

I nodded. "Yes."

Madame Madeline frowned. "I do feel that connection. But there's another connection too. A deeper one. Another man has been important to your mother. And another child too. Was your mother married before? Do you, perhaps, have a sister?"

My jaw dropped. How did she know that? "I *had* a sister," I admitted. "She died."

Madame Madeline looked confused. "Then there must be another one. Another child that your mother is connected to. And you too. I feel these connections very strongly. There's something that separates this child from you, but it isn't death. This connection is so strong that the other child must be alive."

I shook my head. "Sarah died when we were three. We were twins."

"Ah, twins. That's why the connection is so strong."

"Could we please talk about my dad?" I asked. "I haven't heard from him since I was, like, six years old and well, that's sort of why I'm here—"

"I need to hear more about your sister," Madame Madeline interrupted. "Would you mind telling me how she died?"

9

"She drowned."

"I don't think so." Madeline frowned again.

I blinked in surprise. "Yes, she did. I remember."

"You were there?"

"Well, no. But I remember."

Madame Madeline shook her head. "I don't think you do. And I don't think your sister is dead, Samantha. I think she's very much alive."

Chapter 2

"Well, that was bizarre," Angela said as we coasted down the hill on our bikes, our hair flying out behind us. "What a nutcase!"

"Yeah, I guess," I said. I knew Sarah couldn't be alive. She drowned in the old quarry when we were three. That was ten years ago. But what a weird thing for Madame Madeline to say: *I don't think your sister is dead, Samantha. I think she's very much alive.*

"Why would she tell you your sister's alive?" Angela went on. "That just seems mean."

"I don't think she meant to be mean." I started braking as we got near the intersection at the bottom of the hill. "I think she just, I don't know, got her signals crossed or something."

The light was green, so we continued on through the intersection. "What signals?" Angela snorted. "That woman was about as psychic as I am. You should get your money back."

I had to admit Angela was probably right. And I shouldn't have been surprised. I mean, you couldn't expect a real live psychic to live in Clearwater, Iowa. Still, I couldn't help feeling disappointed. I went to Madame Madeline because I wanted her to tell me something about my dad. And she hadn't said a word about him. Not one word.

Angela and I turned onto Center Street. We had to ride single file now, because there was a lot more traffic. As I pedaled, I thought about my dad.

It had been so long since I'd seen him that I could hardly picture him anymore. I knew he was tall and thin and he had hair that was so blond it was practically white. Just like mine. But I couldn't see him in my mind at all.

There were no pictures of him around our house. No nothing of him around our house. All I had left of him was a crumpled-up postcard with a monkey on it that he mailed from the San Diego Zoo when I was six. The note on the back read, "For my Sammy Bear. With love from the Monkey Man."

I never knew for sure why my mom and dad got divorced. Mom told me a long time ago that it was because my dad was irresponsible and childish. But once when Grandma Sperling was visiting from Florida, she told me my parents had never had a good marriage. She said they got married really young and then when Sarah died, their whole marriage fell apart. She also said that the death of a child is the worst thing that can happen to a couple and that lots of people get divorced afterwards.

Angela and I moved to the sidewalk because now there was even more traffic and the road was pretty narrow. The sidewalk was even narrower, though.

I could sort of remember the day Sarah died. My mom would say I couldn't possibly remember that, but I did. It was a day a lot like today. Hot and sticky. And we were all going to go on a picnic. Mom. Dad. Sarah. And me. But I was sick, so I couldn't go. Mom and Dad fought about it. Dad thought I was well enough to go on the picnic, but Mom said no. In the end, she stayed home with me while Dad and Sarah went to the old Clearwater quarry.

Dad took her out on the water in his canoe. I know he shouldn't have done that. You're not supposed to go swimming or boating in the quarry. But he did it anyway. And somehow the canoe tipped over and they fell into the water. My dad tried to save Sarah, but he couldn't.

I don't know what happened after that. I just know that one day my dad went away and he never came back.

Now my mom's getting married again. I can deal with that. Really, I can. The only problem is, they want Bob to adopt me. And I'm not sure I want him to.

What about my real dad? Doesn't he have to give permission or anything?

Mom says he doesn't because he's been gone so long. Nobody knows where he is. Mom says we can do whatever we want because he gave up parenting rights a long time ago.

Well, no one ever asked me what *I* want. I want to find my dad. I want to know what he thinks about some other guy adopting me. And I want to know if he would ever want to be my dad again.

"You look pretty serious," Angela said, riding up beside me. We had turned onto McGregor, which was a quiet, tree-lined residential street, so we were back in the road. I hadn't even realized it.

"What are you thinking about?" Angela asked.

I shrugged. I wasn't much in the mood for talking.

"You still disappointed that that psychic couldn't help you find your father?"

"Sort of."

"You know, Sam..." I could tell Angela was about to say something I wasn't going to like. "Maybe you should just forget about your father and let Bob adopt you."

Let Bob adopt me? She had to be kidding!

"At least he's nice. And I bet he really wants to adopt you. He's not just doing it for your mom."

"But he's not my dad. And I don't want a piece of paper that says he is my dad when he isn't. I've got a real dad out there somewhere."

"Real fathers are overrated, Sam," Angela said. "Look at mine."

Angela's dad wouldn't win any Father of the Year awards, but at least he was part of her life. Sort of. He sent birthday and Christmas gifts. She and her older brother even visited him in Minnesota sometimes. Well, okay, they hadn't visited in a while. But that was because Mr. Hunter and his wife had a baby last year.

"At least you know your dad," I said.

"Father," Angela corrected. "Not dad. And yeah, I know him." Her bike wobbled a little when she said that.

"I know he ran off with some other woman, got married, and had another kid who is tons more important to him than Andrew and I are. He's a selfish jerk. That's what I know about him."

"You know more than that," I pointed out. "You know whether you look like him or talk like him. You know which habits and personality quirks you got from him. You know what he does for a living, what he does in his spare time, what he eats for breakfast. I don't know any of that about my dad."

Angela snorted. "I still say you're better off."

"How?" How could a person *ever* be better off not knowing their dad?

"Because right now, your father could be anyone. Anyone you want him to be. But once you find him, that's it. You're stuck with whoever he is."

"I don't care who he is," I insisted. "He's my dad. That's all that matters."

"That's easy for you to say now when you don't know anything about him. Don't get your hopes up. That's all I'm saying."

I looked away. Sometimes Angela's kind of negative. It's easier for her that way. But me, I try to look on the bright side. I mean, if you don't have hope, what do you have?

* * *

There's a For Sale sign in front of our little blue house on Hartman Lane. My mom and Bob are building a bigger house in one of the new developments, so we're moving after the wedding.

I'll be closer to Angela when we move. I'll have a bigger room with built-in bookshelves, a built-in window seat, and my own bathroom. But I'd still rather stay here. This is my house, you know? It's the only place I've ever lived.

Besides, if my dad ever came looking for me, this is where he'd come. This is where we all lived. But if I had a new name and a new house, how would he ever find me?

I fumbled around in my purse for my house key, then unlocked the front door. Right away my cat padded over to me and meowed.

"Hey, Sherlock," I said, bending to pick him up. The motorboat in his gut revved up as I buried my face in his fur. My cat has the loudest purr of any cat I've ever heard. But I'm not complaining. When cats purr, they're telling you they love you.

I set Sherlock down on the floor and he followed me down the hall. One whole wall in our hallway is lined with pictures. Pictures of me, pictures of Mom, pictures of me and Mom, pictures of me and Mom and Grandma and Grandpa Sperling. The other wall only has two pictures on it—one of me (my eighth-grade school picture) and one of Sarah (age three).

There were other pictures of Sarah in albums somewhere, but this was the only one we had out where people could see it. She's wearing a frilly white dress with a matching ribbon in her hair. She looks shy. She's not smiling very big and she's got her hands folded neatly in her lap.

Somewhere there was a picture of me that looked almost the same (like I said, we were twins), except I was wearing a frilly blue dress instead of a frilly white dress and my smile was way bigger. At one time, that picture probably hung right next to the picture of Sarah. But Mom puts up my new school picture every year. Sarah's picture always stays the same.

Why was I still obsessing about my sister? There was no way she could still be alive. She's out at Lakeview Cemetery right by the big oak tree. End of story.

I headed to my room. Man, was I tired after all that biking. As I flopped down on my bed, I caught a glimpse of my hair in the mirror. It looked like someone had taken a mixer to it. I reached for my brush and immediately went to work.

Sherlock jumped up beside me and meowed. He turned around a couple times, then settled down right next to my favorite stuffed monkey. It's just an old, floppy brown thing. I don't even know where I got it, but it seems like I've always had it. I tickled Sherlock under his chin with the monkey's tail and he purred. Silly cat.

Then I went back to my hair. I'm not sure whether the trip to the psychic was worth this much damage. I don't even know what I was thinking going to see a psychic in the first place. About all I can say about it is it worked in

Who Is Victor Marsh? which was a really good book that I read last week. It was about a woman who was looking for her long-lost brother. The police were looking for him too, because they thought he was a serial killer. But the woman thought they were wrong. She wanted to find her brother before the police did, so she hired this psychic. The psychic not only found the brother, she also found the real killer.

I love books like that. I love all books, but I especially love mysteries. In fact, I think I'd like to be a mystery writer when I grow up.

My mom says I'm dreaming if I think I can make a living as a writer. She can be just as negative as Angela sometimes. I once asked her what was so bad about having dreams and she said, "You can't live on them." Maybe not, but I still think dreams are important.

Slam!

Speak of the devil.

"Hello?" my mom called out. "Sam? Are you home?"

"Yeah," I called back. I put the finishing touches on my hair, then took a quick glance around my room. There wasn't much she could complain about. A few books on the floor. And my nightshirt. I stacked the books on my desk next to my flute case and kicked the nightshirt under my bed.

"Sam!" Mom yelled again from the main part of the house.

"What?" I trotted down to the kitchen.

Mom stood by the sink with her hands on her hips.

She had on her nurse's uniform—white pants, a pastel blue flowery shirt, and white shoes. "Why are the breakfast dishes still sitting in the sink?" she asked.

Oops. "Um, I guess I didn't get around to putting them in the dishwasher," I said.

"Why not?"

I shrugged.

"What did you do all day?" She frowned at the pile of empty boxes that were still stacked in the corner of the kitchen. She had asked me to go down to the basement and start boxing up stuff that we weren't likely to need in the next month, but well...I didn't get to that either.

What could I say? I just shrugged again.

Mom sighed. "Could you at least take care of the dishes before we go?"

"Go?" Where were we going?

"Today's Bob's mother's birthday," Mom said, as though I should have known. "They're having a big party at her house tonight. Everyone's going to be there."

"Everyone," of course, meant Bob's brother and sisters and all their husbands and wives and small children.

I tried not to groan. "Do I have to go?"

"You don't want to?" She sounded surprised.

"Well, it's just that..." I began. It's just that I feel weird around Bob's family. I don't mean they're horrible people. They're okay. But there are so many of them. And they're all so loud and so...I don't know. Just *different* from me.

"It's just that what?" Mom pressed.

I kicked at a crumb on the floor. "Nothing. It's fine. I'll go." It wasn't like she'd let me stay home anyway.

"We'll leave in about an hour," Mom said. "Please try to look presentable."

"So, you want me to leave my nose ring at home?" I was joking. I don't have a nose ring. I have earrings. I wear two in one earlobe and one in the other. But no nose ring, eyebrow ring, tongue ring, belly button ring—nothing like that.

I honestly thought I was being funny. But Mom just walked away, shaking her head.

See, that's the thing about me and my mom. We don't understand each other. We haven't for a long time.

I think the problem is I'm not turning into the person she wants me to be. I'm a person with dreams. She wants me to be a person with "goals." Dreams and goals are not the same thing.

Maybe that was another reason why I wanted to find my dad so bad. I had a feeling I wouldn't have to explain stuff like that to him. He'd just understand.

Chapter 3

Bob's mother lives in the Lyndhurst neighborhood. That's the really old, nice neighborhood near downtown. The houses are big and close together. And the trees are so tall and thick they practically form an umbrella over the whole street.

There were so many cars in front of Bob's mother's house that we had to drive around the corner to park. Mom found a spot in front of a police car. It probably belonged to one of Bob's brothers. Just about everyone in his family is a cop. Bob's dad was a cop too. But he got killed during a robbery or something a long time ago.

Before we got out of the car, Mom put her hand on my arm. "Please try and have a good time, Sam," she said. "In another month, these people are going to be your family."

They're going to be *her* family, not mine. But I just said, "Sure." Whatever.

I tucked in my blouse and smoothed my skirt while Mom carefully picked up the gift-wrapped square box from the back seat. Then I grabbed the mystery I'd been reading and the birthday card I'd whipped up in about ten minutes on our computer before we left, and we trudged back to Bob's mother's house. As soon as we started up the walk, Bob came out onto the porch.

My mom's whole face lit up when she saw him. I have to tell you, for a middle-aged guy, Bob's not bad looking. He's got brown hair like my mom's, blue eyes, and a really nice smile that makes you smile back whether you mean to or not.

Bob's nothing like the cops you see on TV. He's kind of quiet. I can't imagine him ever pulling a gun on anyone and yelling, "Stop! You're under arrest!"

"Hi, hon." Bob bent down and hugged my mom. He glanced at me over her shoulder. "Sam, how are you?"

"Okay."

"Suzanne!" Bob's mother bellowed as she came to the door. She's almost a whole head shorter than I am, but you'd never know it by her voice. People halfway down the block could probably hear her.

My Grandma Sperling is totally different from Bob's mother. She's quiet and reserved. And she wears polyester pantsuits all the time, even when she's just sitting around the condo. Bob's mother wears stained T-shirts that say "If Mom Says No, Ask Grandma." It kind of makes me wonder how these two ladies are going to get along when Grandma and Grandpa Sperling come for the wedding in a few weeks.

"I'm so glad you could come," Bob's mother said, reaching up to hug my mom.

"Me too." My mom hugged her back. "Happy birthday, Mom."

Mom? When did she start calling Bob's mother Mom?

"And Samantha!" I tried not to stiffen when Bob's mother reached out to hug me. "It's nice to see you again."

Bob's mother told me a long time ago that I should call her Grandma. But I don't think of her as Grandma. I think of her as "Bob's mother." I don't want to hurt her feelings, though, so I avoid the whole issue by not calling her anything.

I pasted a cheery smile on my face. "Happy birthday," I said, handing her my card. I held tight to my book with my elbow.

"Thank you, sweetie. You didn't have to make me a card."

Well, yes, actually, I did, but whatever.

I followed my mom into the living room. Something smelled good. Lasagna, I think. One thing I could say for this party, we'd be eating well. The people in Bob's family are excellent cooks.

We don't do a lot of fancy cooking in our family. Mom never makes anything that requires more than ten minutes of effort. And I'm not sure my grandparents even know how to cook. We always eat out when we're with them.

Mom and I wound our way around all the TV trays and toys that were scattered around the living room. There were a bunch of ladies standing around talking and laughing in the kitchen. All the men, except Bob, and all the little kids (the next oldest kid after me is about seven) were running around like maniacs in the backyard.

"Hey, everyone!" Bob's mother announced. "Look who's here." As soon as Bob's sisters and sisters-in-law saw my mom, the hugging started all over again. They're really big on hugging in this family.

I hung back in the living room. My mom looked so happy. So comfortable. Like she was already one of them. Me, I couldn't imagine ever being one of them.

"I see Rick's kids are playing ball out back." Bob touched my arm. "Do you want to go out?"

Bob's really trying here. I know that. He wants us all to be one big, happy family, just like my mom does. But no matter how hard we both try, he and his family are not my family. And going out in the backyard to play with a plastic ball and bat and run around some trees with all those little kids isn't going to change that.

"Thanks," I said, holding up my book. "I think maybe I'll just stay in here and read."

"By yourself?"

I doubted anybody in this family ever did anything by themselves. They weren't readers, either.

I shrugged. "I like to read." Besides, it was kind of hard to play in a skirt.

"Okay." Bob sounded disappointed. "But come and join us if you change your mind."

As soon as he left, I plopped down on the couch. It was one of those poufy couches with lots of pillows that you sort of sink into. I love couches like this. I pulled my feet up under me and opened my book. But I'd barely read two pages before my mom burst into the room. Bob's mother and all his sisters and sisters-in-law were right behind her, all smiles and excitement.

"Guess what, Sam!" Mom said. Her face glowed. "Mom finished your bridesmaid's dress!"

Again with the "Mom." I tried not to react to that. Focus on the dress instead. "She did?"

"Why don't you come try it on so we can see how it fits?" Bob's mother said.

"Okay." I had to admit I was curious about this dress. And I'm always up for trying on clothes. Who wouldn't be? So I set my book down and followed everyone up to Bob's mother's bedroom. I had to dodge a bunch of cars and stuffed animals along the way. Geez, you'd think ten kids lived here instead of one lady.

"Oh, my goodness!" Mom clasped her hands to her cheeks when she saw the blue dress that hung on a hanger over the back of the bedroom door. Everyone else oohed and aahed too.

I was pretty amazed myself. I'd seen the shiny blue fabric my mom had picked out. And I'd seen the dress pattern. But seeing the whole thing together for the first time... Wow! I didn't know what to say.

"Do you like it?" Mom asked me.

"Oh, yeah. Definitely." Mom and I hardly ever have the same taste in clothes, but I did like this dress. It was simple, but elegant. There was no lace, just smooth taffeta. You could wear it on the shoulders or off, but if I knew my mom, I'd be wearing it up.

Bob's mother carefully took the dress down from the hanger. "Let's see how it looks on you," she said, holding it out to me.

She didn't expect me to actually get undressed in front of all these people, did she? I didn't mind my mom being there, but I don't like to undress in front of strangers.

"You did a great job on this, Mom," one of the sisters or sisters-in-law said as she ran her finger along the smooth skirt.

"You sure did," my mom agreed. She unzipped the dress. "Come on, Sam," she said impatiently. "Try it on."

Apparently no one was leaving. I kicked my shoes off, slid my skirt down, and unbuttoned my blouse. Unfortunately, I wasn't wearing a strapless bra, so I had to take my regular old bra off. I tried to cover up a little.

Mom sighed. "Move your arms, Sam. How are we going to get a dress on when your arms are crossed?"

I moved my arms. Then my mom and Bob's mother carefully eased the dress over my head. It made kind of a crinkly, swishy sound as it dropped into place. I reached back to lift my hair, then looked down. The dress flared out around my knees.

"Oh, Sam." My mom had tears in her eyes.

I turned to look at myself in the mirror and my eyeballs nearly popped out of my head. I looked so *different*. Older, definitely. But sort of mature too. Like I'd had all these huge life experiences or something.

Mom gathered my hair and held it on top of my head.

"Here. You hold your hair and I'll zip you up," she said.

The dress tightened around my chest as the zipper went up.

"You look..." Mom stopped. She was at a loss for words.

"She looks absolutely breathtaking," Bob's mother said.

Breathtaking? Me?

"Yes, she does," the sisters-in-law all agreed.

Bob's mother had me climb up on a chair so she could pin the hem. Then they all started talking about what a beautiful wedding it was going to be and how nice it was that Grandpa Sperling was coming all the way from Florida to walk Mom down the aisle.

Even though it was a second marriage for my mom, it was a first marriage for Bob, so they were going all out on the ceremony. Plus my mom and dad never had a formal wedding. They just got married in the courthouse. Mom says that if she does the wedding up right this time, maybe the marriage will work out better.

I do hope this marriage works out. Really, I do. I want my mom to be happy. But...I want to be happy too. Is that so wrong? And the one thing that could really, truly make me happy would be finding my dad.

Chapter 4

On Thursday morning, I finished the book I was reading, fixed my hair, practiced my flute, and then, because it was too stormy outside to do anything else, I actually did what my mom wanted me to do. I took a bunch of empty boxes down to our dingy old laundry/storage room in the basement and started boxing up random stuff that was piled on the shelves. Stuff we probably wouldn't need until after we moved like the blender, the Crock-Pot, and extra Tupperware. I hoped my mom wouldn't decide two days from now that she needed some of this stuff after all. But at least she couldn't complain that I never made any effort around here.

I hated this room. It was dark and gloomy. The only light came from a single lightbulb that hung from the ceiling in the middle of the room. The whole place smelled like old, wet rags. Probably because the only "carpet" down here was a big rug that really was made from old rags. I think it was my grandma's. Plus, there were spiders. Tons of them.

I could hear the low rumble of thunder and the *plink plink plink* of rain against the little window above my head. The bulb flickered, but it didn't go out. So, I kept working. My cat Sherlock watched from under the ironing board.

Once I cleared the shelves by the washer and dryer, I moved on to the ones across from the deep freeze. Most of the stuff over here was already boxed up. I probably didn't have to do anything with it, but I pulled out one of the boxes and peeked inside just to see what was there. It was full of old Barbie stuff.

I smiled. I used to love Barbies. Playing Barbies was one of the few things I remembered doing with my sister. In fact, I could even remember my mom getting down on the floor and playing with us too. She was fun then. We'd dress all the Barbies in fancy clothes, then send them to Cinderella's ball. Wow. I had no idea my mom, Ms. Let's-Go-Through-the-House-and-Get-Rid-of-Stuff, saved all this. Who knew what else was down here?

I shoved that box back where I found it and pulled out another. This one was a lot heavier. I had to pull hard to get it out. When I opened it up, I discovered it was full of old Dr. Seuss books. *The Cat in the Hat. Hop on Pop. Green Eggs and Ham.*

There were more boxes way in the back. Unlike the ones in front, these were all sealed up with several layers of strong packing tape. I ran upstairs to get a sharp knife, then came back down. There was so much tape on the one box, it was hard to cut through. But eventually I got through it all and yanked open the flaps. Inside were a few award ribbons that belonged to my mom, a dried corsage, and an old Clearwater High School yearbook.

Well, this could be interesting. I pulled out the year-book and looked up Suzanne Sperling in the index. I wondered how dorky my mom looked in high school. It turned out she looked pretty much the same as she does now. Same hairstyle and everything. My mom was in band, yearbook, cross country (my mom ran cross country?), and Future Scientists of America. That was even more surprising than the cross country.

I knew my mom and dad graduated from high school together. They were in the same class, even though Dad was a year older. With trembling fingers I flipped ahead to the W's. But there was no Joseph Wright listed. The W's went from Terry Warner to David Wyatt. After all the senior portraits, there was a list of students not pictured: Michelle Mallory, Samuel Roth, and Joseph Wright. Why was I not surprised? I wasn't sure I'd ever seen a picture of my dad.

I started packing everything back into the box when I realized I'd almost missed a small black velvet box like the kind you get from a jewelry store. I opened it up and just about choked. Inside was a ring. A *wedding* ring? Yes, I was pretty sure that's what it was. It had a simple gold band with a diamond sticking up. Was this the ring my mom wore when she and my dad were married?

I was about to lift the ring out of the velvet casing and take a closer look when…*ding dong!* The sound of the doorbell startled me so much I almost dropped the box. I set it down, then dashed up the stairs two at a time.

I opened the front door and found Angela standing

on my front porch. She was wearing a soaking wet yellow raincoat. Her hair hung in wet curls around her shoulders.

"Hey," I said, opening the screen door to let her in.

"Hey yourself." She stomped her feet on the doormat and water splattered all over my feet. "Get your shoes and coat. It's a great day to go to the mall!"

I stared at the sheets of rain pounding the driveway. "You want to go to the mall now?" Both our moms were working, so there was no one to drive us. We'd have to walk. In the pouring rain.

"Why not?" She grinned. "Ben Willard might be there."

I could feel my face heating up. Ben Willard is so cute. He used to have this thick curly hair, but he got a buzz cut for the summer. Ben and his friends hung out at Tilt, which was this place at the mall with old pinball machines and video games. But it wasn't like they ever noticed us. And to tell you the truth, I wasn't sure I wanted them to notice us if we were going to walk a mile and a half in the pouring rain.

"I don't know," I said. "I'm kind of busy."

"Busy? Doing what?"

"Come on. I'll show you."

Angela slipped off her raincoat, kicked off her shoes, then followed me downstairs.

I showed her the ring. She took it out of the box and held it up to the light to inspect it. "Nice."

"I think it's my mom's old wedding ring."

"Really?" Angela squinted. "Is it engraved?"

"I don't know," I said. "I just found it before you got here." I scanned the inside the gold band while Angela held it between her thumb and forefinger. I didn't see any engraving.

"My mom's ring says, 'Always, Tom.'" Angela snorted as she handed the ring back. "What a joke!"

I returned the ring to the velvet box, put it back inside the big cardboard box, then looked around for some tape to seal it back up.

"You found a diamond ring packed away in an old box down here?" Angela asked.

"Yup." Unfortunately, I couldn't find any tape, so I just folded the flaps under one another and lifted the box back to the shelf I found it on.

"My mom doesn't wear her old wedding ring, either," Angela said as she sat cross-legged on the floor. "But she keeps it in a dresser drawer. Not in a box in the basement."

"Well, I'm surprised my mom kept her ring at all. She got rid of everything else that had to do with my dad. Pictures. Videos. Everything."

"Everything?" Angela asked, wide-eyed.

"Everything."

"Wow, she must really hate him."

"Yeah," I said. "I guess so."

Angela leaned back against the washer and stretched her legs out in front of her. "So, what are you going to do about your mom if you actually find your dad?" she asked.

I pulled out another box. "What do you mean?"

"Well, what will you tell your mom? She's not just going to smile and say 'Oh, how nice for you,' you know. Do you think she'll let you see him?"

I had to admit, I hadn't thought about that.

"I don't know," I said, resting my elbows on the box. "Maybe I won't tell her. Maybe I'll just go run away and live with him."

"What?" Angela cried. "You don't even *know* him. How do you know you'd want to live with him?"

I shrugged. "He's my dad. Why wouldn't I want to live with him? I doubt my mom would miss me anyway. She's got Bob. I'm old enough to choose, don't you think?"

"I don't know. Doesn't your mom have custody? I don't think you can just decide to go live with your dad."

"You should be able to when you're thirteen," I said as I plunged my knife into the tape on the box in front of me.

Angela crossed her legs. "You know, you've never really told me much about your dad," she said. "What do you remember about him?"

"Not much." I lifted the flaps on the box.

"What kind of job did he have when he was married to your mom?"

"I don't know. I don't think he worked much."

"Why not?"

"I have no idea. I think he wanted to be a musician." Somebody, I don't remember who, had told me that. "Maybe he was waiting for his big break or something."

"A musician?" Angela raised her eyebrow. "Cool! What did he play?"

"I don't think he played anything. I think he just sang." I smiled. "I remember he used to take all these songs that everybody knows and he'd change the words. Like that muffin man song. He used to sing, 'Do you know the monkey man, the monkey man, the monkey man? Do you know the monkey man, who lives on Hartman Lane?'"

Angela giggled. "Sorry, Sam, but you did *not* inherit your father's musical talent."

I stuck my tongue out at her. "Never said I did." I turned my attention to the box in front of me. I lifted the flaps. A single dried pink rose lay right on top.

Oh. My. Gosh.

I suddenly flashed back to a time when I was a really little kid and I was holding my stuffed monkey and all these grown-ups were milling around crying and...there were pink roses all over the house.

Sarah's funeral.

"What's the matter?" Angela asked.

I couldn't answer her. I felt like the floor had dropped out underneath me. Mom and I didn't talk about my dad very often, but we *never* talked about Sarah.

I set the dried-out flower aside, then checked to see what else was in the box. It looked like old photo albums. I lifted the top album out and opened it up.

"Is that you and your sister?" Angela pointed at a snapshot of two little girls dressed in identical pink dresses standing in front of a white house.

I slid the photo out of the plastic holder to get a closer look. It had to have been taken right before Sarah died. We both looked a lot like that picture of her that hung in our hallway. We had wispy white blond hair that touched our shoulders. Neither of us was smiling. In fact, we both looked a little worried. Like maybe we sensed that something bad was about to happen.

"Which one's you?" Angela asked.

I squinted first at one girl, then the other. "I—I don't know." It felt weird that I couldn't tell. But each girl was an exact copy of the other. It was like someone took a picture of a house, then photoshopped the same little kid into the picture twice.

"There are some old newspapers in here too." Angela reached into the box and pulled out a small stack of newspaper pages that had been folded over and tied with a string.

I slipped the photo into my jeans pocket, then took the stack from Angela. I slid the string off and gasped as I realized what the articles were about.

"These are all about the drowning."

"Let me see." Angela leaned over and we read the first article together. The headline was missing.

CLEARWATER—An afternoon at the Clearwater quarry turned tragic for a father and daughter last night. Joseph

Wright, 23, of Clearwater, told police that he and his daughter Sarah, 3, had been canoeing at the quarry. The canoe capsized and Wright unsuccessfully searched the dark, murky water for his daughter. Jonathan Avery, 35, of Cedar Rapids and his wife Joanne, 32, told police that they were out walking at the quarry when they saw someone fall into the water. A child's life preserver was found in the canoe, but so far divers have been unable to recover the body. The water depth in some parts of the quarry can reach up to three hundred feet. "We hope Sarah somehow managed to get to shore and is out there somewhere, waiting to be found," the missing child's mother, Suzanne Wright, also 23, said late last night. Ms. Wright also reported that her daughter did not know how to swim. The search for Sarah Wright is expected to resume today.

"Wow," Angela said.

"Yeah. Wow." I felt somehow removed from this story. Like this was an article about some other family instead of my own. That quote didn't even sound like my mom. She sounded...emotional. Emotional is not a word I'd use to describe my mom.

"Here's another one," I said, setting the first article aside.

> —The search continues for three-year-old Sarah Wright of Clearwater. Sarah was last seen on Thursday afternoon at the Clearwater quarry when the canoe she and her father were in capsized. A crew from Cedar Rapids has been dragging the quarry since Thursday, but according to Capt. Jim Morgan of the Linn County sheriff's office, the search has been unsuccessful. "The truth is," he said, "we have no idea where little Sarah's body might be."

That article had a picture of my mom and dad. Finally, an actual photo with my dad in it. I peered hard at the newspaper clipping.

He looked young for a parent. So did my mom, for that matter. They were standing in front of a red truck and my dad was wearing blue jeans and a plain white T-shirt. He had really light hair that covered his ears, a thick mustache, and a pointy nose, kind of like mine. I ran my finger across his nose. *Where are you, Dad?* I thought as I stared into his eyes. *Why haven't you been in touch in all these years?*

"What do the other articles say?" Angela asked.

I set that article aside and picked up the next one. It didn't really say anything new. In fact, as I skimmed through the whole pile of articles, I noticed they all sounded the same until we got to Sarah's obituary. Then it was like, this is it. The end. Sarah's dead. The final line of the obituary really drove the point home. "Sarah is survived by one sister, Samantha, also age 3."

Except...there was something missing. Something that surely should have been mentioned in at least one of these articles...I flipped back through them again, reading each one more thoroughly this time. Had I just missed it before?

"What are you looking for?" Angela asked.

"Shh!" I had to concentrate.

But when I got to the end of the pile, I still hadn't found it.

I looked at Angela. "Did you notice that every one of those articles talked about this big search they were doing for Sarah? Every one of them either begins or ends with, 'the search continues.' But there's nothing in here that says when or where her body was found," I said.

"Maybe it wasn't found?" Angela suggested.

A little chill crept up my back when she said that.

The psychic lady's words came back to me: *I don't think your sister is dead, Samantha. I think she's very much alive.*

"Maybe it wasn't," I said slowly.

Angela looked a little confused.

I went on, "What if that psychic was right? What if Sarah's body was never found because...she's not dead?"

"Whoa." Angela's eyes seemed to grow to the size of golf balls.

"I know there's a gravestone out at Lakeside Cemetery, but that doesn't mean there's anyone buried there," I said. "This is kind of creepy, but my Grandma and Grandpa Sperling have gravestones. I think you can buy one whenever you want."

Angela opened her mouth to say something, then closed it. When she finally opened it again, she said, "Listen to me, Sam. Nobody buys a gravestone for a little kid unless that little kid is dead."

"Maybe everyone just thinks she's dead, but really she's not?"

Angela frowned. "Well, if she's not dead, where is she? Where has she been all this time?"

"I don't know." I flipped through the articles until I came to the first one we'd read. "My mom said 'we hope she somehow managed to get to shore.' Maybe she did. Maybe somebody found her. Somebody who wasn't from around here. Maybe they took her home and raised her as their own kid."

Angela wrinkled her nose. "Don't you think that sounds a little Hallmark Channel? How would she have gotten to shore? She was three years old. She couldn't swim."

"Maybe she could."

Angela grabbed the article and held it in front of my face. "Your mom said she couldn't. Listen to me, Sam. That quarry is huge. And it's really deep. If your sister's body was never found, it's because there was too much water. Not because she somehow survived."

"You don't know that for sure," I said.

I could tell Angela thought I had gone totally crazy, but I've read enough detective novels to know that until the detective finds the body, it's almost impossible for the DA to prove murder. That's because without a body, there's still a chance, even a really small one, that the person is actually alive.

Angela cocked her head at me. "Do you honestly believe your sister's still alive, Sam?"

Did I? I looked down at the articles in my lap. "I don't know. It's possible."

"No way." Angela shook her head.

But as far as I was concerned, the only way it *wasn't* possible was if Sarah's body was buried in her gravesite at Lakeview Cemetery. And that was easy enough to find out. All I had to do was ask my mom.

Chapter 5

"Look alive out there, Wright!" Coach Frye called as the ball sailed over my head. It had stopped storming right after lunch and now the sun was out. That meant we had practice that day.

Too bad.

Softball is not exactly my sport. I'm not sure I have a sport. I probably should've done my team a favor and not gone out for softball this summer. But Angela really wanted to play, so I figured I might as well play too. The thing is, Angela's actually good at softball. But me? I get a hit maybe once every three or four times I'm up at bat, and I can't catch or throw for anything. Just ask Bob. He saw me play a few weeks ago and right afterward, he politely offered to give me a few pointers. But hey, it's just a game, right? So what if I'm bad at it?

I scurried after the ball and threw it to our pitcher, Marianna Detert, but it went a little short. Ashley Frye shook her head like she couldn't believe how bad I was. She grabbed the ball and lobbed it underhand to Marianna.

By then the runner for the Central City team was already home.

"Sorry," I called out. I'll admit I was even more off than usual today. I just couldn't stop thinking about those newspaper articles. And Sarah. Was I crazy to think there was a chance my sister was still alive?

"Look out, Sam! Fly ball!" Angela shouted.

Before I could react, something whacked me hard in the forehead and knocked me to the ground.

"Sam? Sam? Are you okay?" someone asked. The ground trembled as everyone ran toward me.

I closed my eyes and let the back of my head rest on the ground. My whole head throbbed. A lot.

"Sam?" Coach Frye patted my cheek. "Can you hear me, Sam?"

My eyelids fluttered open and I peered into a sea of concerned faces.

"She's not unconscious," Ashley noted.

"No, but she's going to have quite a goose egg in the middle of her forehead," Coach Frye said.

I'm not sure if I groaned out of pain or self-pity. Just what I needed. A goose egg in the middle of my forehead.

"Are you okay, Sam?" Coach Frye asked.

"I think so," I said, trying to sit up. I blinked a few times.

"Are you dizzy?" Coach Frye asked.

"I—I don't know." Ow! It felt like someone had closed a waffle iron around my head. I felt for the bump on my forehead. It was already about the size of an egg.

Coach Frye helped me to the bench. Angela brought me an ice pack and Coral Wilson offered me two Tylenol. The girls from the Central City team all stood around like they were bored.

"I think we'd better call your mom," Coach Frye said, pulling out his phone.

"Okay. Wait...what time is it?"

He checked his phone. "About five thirty."

"I...I don't think you'll be able to reach her." I touched my head gently. "She should...be on her way home from work...and she never answers her phone when she's driving."

"Is there somebody else we could call? A friend or relative? I think somebody needs to know that you've been injured. Who's your emergency contact?" He reached for the clipboard with all our emergency sheets.

I had a feeling Bob was my emergency contact. And I sure didn't want Coach Frye to call him.

"You don't have to call anyone," I said quickly. "It really doesn't hurt all that much. And the game's almost over. I can just sit here and rest until Angela's mom picks us up."

Coach Frye checked my forehead again and frowned. "Well, just take it easy, okay? I don't like to mess around with head injuries."

I spent the rest of the time sitting on the bench with an ice pack pressed to my forehead. Which, aside from the pain, wasn't a bad way to spend a softball game.

* * *

"What happened to you?" Mom asked the second I walked into the kitchen. She was rinsing grapes in the sink.

"It's that obvious?" I moaned. Angela and Coral had helped me arrange my bangs after practice. Coral said the bump wasn't really that noticeable. I should've known she was just being nice.

Mom turned off the water and came over to get a better look at me.

"Ow!" I cried when she moved my bangs.

"Did you get hit by a ball?"

"Yes." I eased myself into a chair. "But it's not a big deal." And I didn't want to talk about it. "Mom, there's something else we need talk about. Something important."

"Mmm?" Mom poked at the area around my bump.

I pushed her hand away. "I was going through some boxes in the basement earlier today. And I found one that had a bunch of stuff about Sarah in it. Old photos and newspaper articles and stuff."

Mom froze. She literally froze in place. But then she said, "We should probably get some ice on that bump," totally ignoring what I'd just said.

"Did you hear me?" I asked.

Mom pulled a dish towel out of the drawer, then grabbed a handful of ice cubes from the freezer. "Yes." She wadded the towel around the ice. "I just think we should take care of that bump on your head now."

"I had ice on it for twenty minutes."

"Good." Mom put the towel of ice in my hand, then moved my hand to my forehead. "Now you can sit for another twenty minutes. You'll thank me for this tomorrow when the swelling's gone down."

I sighed, but kept the ice against my forehead. "There was a lot of stuff in those articles downstairs about how everybody was searching for Sarah," I tried again. "But there wasn't anything in there about her body being found."

"Please, Sam," Mom said, walking back to the sink. "It's been a long day. I really don't want to talk about this now." She turned the water back on and rinsed the grapes some more.

"But you'll never want to talk about it," I said. "We never talk about Sarah."

Mom turned off the water again. Was her hand actually shaking?

She leaned against the sink to steady herself for a few seconds, then she slowly turned to look at me. "No, I guess we don't," she said finally. "It's been ten years, but it's still hard for me to talk about her."

I lowered my eyes. "I—I just want to know about those articles in the newspaper," I said. I didn't want to get into a huge thing with Mom. But I had to know. "Why wasn't there one that said her body was found?"

Mom pressed her lips together, then blinked up at the ceiling a few times. A couple of seconds later, she came over and sank down into the chair beside me. "Because her body wasn't ever found," she said quietly.

"It wasn't?" I knew it!

"No."

"How come you never told me?"

"I don't know. It wasn't important—"

"Wasn't *important?*" I cried.

Mom slumped back in her chair and rubbed the back of her neck. "It was all so long ago. And you were awfully young."

"I was three. That's old enough to remember some stuff."

Mom looked at me. "You remember Sarah?"

"Of course," I answered immediately. Then I said, "Well, sort of." I wished I remembered *more.*

I reached over and grabbed a banana from the middle of the table. I wasn't really hungry, but peeling it gave me something to do with my hands. "Do you ever think she might still be alive?" I asked.

"No." Mom said firmly.

"Why not?" I set the banana down again. "If Sarah's body was never found, isn't there at least a chance she's alive? Maybe she swam to shore and someone found her and took her? Maybe they raised her as their own child? I read a book about that once. Or maybe she ended up at the police station and the police thought she was someone else, so they gave her to the wrong people?"

It was possible, wasn't it?

Mom shook her head. "I had a hard time accepting

the fact that Sarah was gone," she said. "It's one of the reasons I don't talk about her. Believe me, I came up with all the scenarios you've just described and more. But she's gone, Sam. She's…dead."

"How can you be so sure?" I asked.

"Because of where it happened," Mom said softly. "That quarry is two miles long. It's three hundred feet deep in some places. There's heavy construction equipment and who knows what else at the bottom—"

"You mean under the water?" I asked in disbelief.

"Yes," Mom said. "I think it was left there from when they stopped mining the quarry. The people who searched for Sara in the water couldn't even dive down that far. It was too dangerous."

"Still," I said, staring at the tablecloth. "Without a body, isn't it *possible* Sarah survived?"

Mom shook her head sadly. "No, Sam."

My chest tightened. The thought of someone, anyone, drowning in three hundred feet of murky water—her body drifting down, down, down to a graveyard of abandoned construction equipment—made me feel like I was drowning too.

"I know it's hard without a body," Mom said. "That's why we held a funeral and I bought a memorial marker. I needed closure."

Closure? It sounded to me as though Mom just gave up. She decided Sarah was dead and that was it.

"I'm sorry you had to come across all those articles, honey," Mom said. "By yourself. I didn't even realize they were in those boxes down there. But maybe it's good that the subject did come up. You and I are closing the door on this chapter of our lives. Bob and I will be married soon and we'll all be living in a whole new house. It's time to look forward and put the past behind us."

Easy for Mom to say. I had feeling it was a lot easier to put an ex-husband behind you than a father and a sister.

Chapter 6

I had absolutely no motivation for doing anything that night. I didn't even feel like reading. All I did was stare out my bedroom window. I saw Mrs. Sandvick's two grandsons, Ryan and Josh, splashing in the little kiddie pool on her patio next door. Ryan was four, Josh was five. They lived in California and they had two turtles and a lizard, and they were here for the whole summer because their parents were backpacking in Europe. I learned all that and more one day when Mrs. Sandvick asked me to babysit for them.

Watching those two brothers splash and play made me think of my own sister. I reached into my pocket and pulled out the photo of Sarah and me that I'd found in the basement. I stared at it and thought about how much Sarah and I had missed not growing up together.

As twins, we would've been best friends, I was sure of it. We would've shared a bedroom and stayed up half the night whispering secrets to one another. When we were younger, we probably would've dressed alike, but we would've given that up when we started middle school.

We totally would've had the same taste in clothes, though, so we could've traded clothes once we stopped dressing alike. We probably would have had a lot of the same tastes. But not in boys. We never would've competed for the same boys.

Thinking about Sarah so much was making me depressed. I've always known I had a sister who died, but I never really thought much about it before. Not like this. But ever since I found those articles it seemed like I couldn't stop thinking about Sarah and how things could have been.

I needed to get my mind on something else. I slipped the photo inside one of my books and slid the book under my bed. Then I wandered down the hall to see what my mom was doing. From the kitchen window I spotted Bob's silver Saturn parked in our driveway. He came over almost every night now, but he and my mom never really did much. They watched TV or played board games or worked on this 3-D puzzle of Camelot, which was what they were doing now.

Bob's really into 3-D puzzles. He says they relax him. They prove there is order in the universe. You look at the pieces and match up the pictures. And when you're done you end up with this perfect little miniature of some famous building. I bet it was the order-in-the-universe thing that made my mom fall in love with him in the first place. She's into order.

Anyway, Bob brought over the Camelot puzzle a couple weeks ago and my mom set up a card table in the corner of our living room. They've been building the thing off and on ever since.

I don't think they saw me standing there in the doorway. Every time one of them put two pieces together they'd lean toward each other and kiss.

"These two don't go together," Bob said, pulling two pieces apart.

Mom shrugged. "Do you want your kiss back?"

"I think so." Bob guided my mom out of her chair and into his lap and they started going at it like a couple of high school kids. I could hardly believe it. Who knows what might have happened if I hadn't cleared my throat right then.

They both jumped.

"Sam!" Bob said, all embarrassed.

My mom wiped her mouth on the back of her hand and they pulled away from each other real quick.

"Should I leave?" I asked. Was this what it was going to be like when they were married?

"No!" Mom said sharply.

"Absolutely not," Bob said. He leaped up and pulled out a chair for me. "In fact, why don't you join us?"

Join them? He had to be kidding.

"Yes, you like puzzles, Sam," Mom said, fluffing her hair. "Sit down."

I stared at my mother. *I like puzzles?* When was the last time she saw me put a puzzle together? In fact, when had she *ever* seen me put a puzzle together?

They both shoved piles of puzzle pieces toward me.

Bob peered closer at me. "What's that on your forehead?"

I touched my fingers to the bump on my forehead. "Nothing," I said, flipping my bangs over it. "I got hit by a ball at softball practice, that's all."

"You're supposed to catch with your mitt, not your forehead," Bob said, smiling.

Ha ha. What a funny guy my mom was marrying.

"Hey." Bob elbowed me in the ribs. "That was what my dad said to me when I got hit in the head with a baseball. I didn't find it amusing, either." Then he told us all about how it was the last game of the season and he was standing in the outfield waiting for the batter to hit one when this beautiful red-tailed hawk sailed by overhead. While Bob was watching the hawk, this kid who'd never gotten a hit all season whacked the ball out to left field, where it promptly hit Bob in the head.

My mom smiled at Bob and patted his arm. I could tell she was enjoying this little family moment. She probably hoped Bob and I would bond over our shared ball injuries. But his story didn't change anything between us. He was still the same old Bob. I was still the same old Sam. And the only thing we had in common was my mom.

I was relieved when my phone buzzed with a text from Angela: **Can you FaceTime?**

Sure, I texted back, relieved to have an excuse to get away from the happy couple. **Give me a minute.**

"Where are you going?" Mom called to me as I headed for my room.

"To talk to Angela."

Mom muttered something in response, but I just kicked my bedroom door closed and flopped on my bed next to Sherlock. He didn't look at all happy about being disturbed. Then I called Angela.

"What's up?" I said as soon as her face appeared on my screen. She was sitting on her bed too, but it looked like she was talking to me on her laptop rather than her phone.

"I talked to my father this afternoon," Angela said. "Andrew and I are supposed to go visit him next week."

A hollow spot opened in my chest. "Wow, that's great," I said, trying to sound happy for her.

But she didn't look very happy herself. "Do you know how long it's been since I've seen my father, Sam?"

I thought back. She didn't see him last summer. And I didn't think she saw him the summer before that, either.

"Three years, Sam. Three *years!* What kind of father doesn't see his kids for three years?" She gaped at me.

I couldn't answer that. It had been a lot longer than that since I'd seen my dad.

Sherlock butted his head up against my hand, so I gave his head a little scratch.

"And it's not like Hill Valley is even that far away," Angela went on.

All I knew about Hill Valley was it was in Minnesota and it was where Angela used to live before her parents got divorced and she moved here in second grade.

"Well, at least you get to see him now," I said. She was so lucky.

"I don't know. What's the point? It's not like he actually wants us to come."

I couldn't understand why she had to be so negative all the time. "He wouldn't have invited you if he didn't want you to come," I pointed out.

"He didn't invite us. My mom called him up and told him he had to see us this summer. She was in her room, but I heard her. She said he had to let us come sometime before the summer was over or else."

"Or else what?"

"I don't know. All I know is he's supposed to have us a week at Christmas and two weeks during the summer. But for the last three years he's always had some excuse. First he and what's-her-face eloped, then they had some trip, then she got pregnant, then the baby was born, and he's always going to some medical convention or another. But he's used up all his excuses. My mom said pick a week, and he picked next week. Never mind that I have two softball games and Andrew's supposed to work. He picked next week, so we have to go. Whether we want to or not."

It wasn't fair. Angela didn't want to see her dad, but she had to go anyway. I wanted to see my dad more than anything, and I probably never would. I was so jealous I could hardly see straight. But I swallowed that jealousy down and said, "It won't be as terrible as you think, Angela. You'll see. You'll get to know each other again. You'll probably have a great time."

"I'll have a miserable time," Angela argued. "But so

will our father and what's-her-name, his new wife. We'll all get to be miserable together. Let's talk about something else. How's your forehead? Does it hurt a lot?" She squinted like she was trying to see my bump through her screen.

"No, it's okay. But guess what? I talked to my mom about all those articles and stuff we found in the basement this morning." I told Angela what my mom had said about Sarah's body never being found.

"Really," Angela said.

"Yeah," I said glumly. "But my mom says there's no way Sarah could still be alive."

"Well, of course not," Angela said. "That quarry's pretty deep."

"I know," I said with a heavy sigh.

Angela was right. I knew in my head that there was no way Sarah could still be alive. But still my heart wanted to believe that she was.

Chapter 7

Someone was calling me. "S-a-a-am...S-a-a-am..."

It was dark out. Really dark, and cold too. I could see my breath every time I breathed out.

"S-a-a-am..."

I shivered as I turned all around. "Sarah? Is that you?"

"Yes. Sa-a-am, come here..." The voice trailed away.

"Where are you?" I didn't even know where I was, much less where she was. I knew I was on some dirt path, surrounded by trees. I could hear water in the distance. But I didn't know where we were and I couldn't see anything.

"Please, Sam..."

"I'm trying!" I opened my eyes as wide as they would go and groped around in the darkness, terrified I would run into something. "It's too dark. Where are you?"

"I'm right he-eere..."

Where? I tried to follow her voice, but I couldn't tell where it was coming from.

"Are you by the water?"

"Yes."

"Okay. Hang on, Sarah. I'm coming!" I started running,

my bare feet slapping against the hard ground. There were sharp rocks and sticks in my path, but my sister needed me. I had to keep going.

Then my foot caught the bottom of this strange nightgown I was wearing. My hands and knees hit the ground. Hard.

Tears stung my eyes. "Where are you?" I cried, pounding my fists into the dirt.

"I told you, I'm right here! Hurry, Sam! Hurry!"

I clambered to my feet. I didn't know which way to go.

"Where?" I cried desperately. "Where are you?"

"Over here..."

The trees parted and I found myself at the edge of a lake. Finally, I saw her: My sister. She was my age and she had on a long white nightgown just like mine. Her white-blond hair fanned out around her shoulders. She looked exactly like me.

She was way out in the lake, standing—no, floating—just above the water. She reached out her hand for me. "Come with me, Sam."

But I couldn't go to her. I couldn't stand on top of the water like she could. If I tried, I would surely drown. "No, you come over here," I called to her.

"I can't, Sa-a-am. You have to come to me..." She was drifting further away.

"No," I cried. "Don't go! Don't leave me here!"

"Come with me, Sa-a-am...ple-e-ease..." She was almost gone.

"Sarah! Sarah!" I screamed.

"Sam?" I felt a hand on my shoulder.

I turned and a bright light shone in my face. I covered my eyes with my hands. But my hands were...*wet.* So were my knees.

"Samantha? Are you all right?" someone asked.

I slowly lowered my hands. I was on my knees. In a body of water. But it wasn't a lake, it was a pool. A little kid's inflatable backyard pool. And the light in my face was a back porch light.

"Wake up, Sam." My mom was shaking my arm.

"Is she all right, Suzanne?" Mrs. Sandvick called from her back porch.

By then it was starting to make sense. I was in the Sandvicks's yard next door. This was their kiddie pool.

How incredibly embarrassing!

I wasn't wearing any long, white nightgown. Instead I had on my usual navy nightshirt that barely covered my butt. I leapt away from both the pool and my mother and tried to pull my nightshirt down a little farther, but it didn't stretch as far as I wanted it to. Luckily at this time of night the only people up were me, my mom, and Mrs. Sandvick. And Mrs. Sandvick's eyes probably weren't real good.

"She's fine, Mrs. Sandvick, thanks." Mom waved at our neighbor. "She just had a bad dream and sleepwalked out here."

A bad dream? It was all just a dream? Sarah wasn't calling me?

Of course she wasn't. She drowned ten years ago.

But it had all seemed so *real.*

"Come on, Sam." Mom put her arm around me and led me back to our house.

"Get some sleep, Suzanne," Mrs. Sandvick called. "You too, Samantha."

Mom held the back door for me. "You haven't sleep-walked in years, honey," she said as I stepped into our kitchen.

Huh? "I used to sleepwalk?" I didn't know that.

"When you were little," she told me. "It usually happened when you were upset about something. Are you upset about...you know, what we talked about earlier?"

I turned away. "No, no. I'm not upset," I said. I went to the cabinet and reached for a glass.

"Good," Mom said as I poured myself a glass of water. "Because there's no reason you should be. That all happened a long time ago."

"I know," I said. But if it was so long ago, why did the pain feel so fresh?

* * *

"Angela! Sam!" Coral waved to us.

It was Tuesday afternoon and Angela and I had decided to go to the water park.

Dodging towels and moms and little kids, we made our way around the splash pool and found a spot over by Coral and some other girls we knew from school. They had claimed a group of lounge chairs by the deep pool, in perfect view of Kyle Jenkins, a cute sophomore who was lifeguarding today.

There weren't any chairs left, so Angela and I spread

out our towels on the ground next to Tara Huntley and Melissa Holt. We all slathered suntan lotion on each other's backs and combed our hair and talked. Angela told everyone about her upcoming trip to visit her father. Coral complained about her mom. And for the zillionth time, Melissa repeated the story of her big breakup with Dylan Kane. The girl was never going to get over it.

While Melissa was talking I noticed a little girl in the pool. She had on a one-piece swimming suit with a big pink fish on her stomach. And a memory came to me, clear as anything. *Sarah had a swimsuit with a big pink fish on it.* I had one just like it, only my fish was yellow, and I liked hers better—

"Earth to Sam." Coral waved her hand in front of my face.

I blinked. My friends were all staring at me.

"What?" I tucked my hair behind my ear.

Melissa shifted on her towel and rolled her eyes like it was a big deal for her to repeat herself. "I *said,* I heard your mom's getting married."

"Oh. Yeah. Next month." The little girl with the fish suit climbed out of the pool, then cannonballed back in with a big splash.

"Do you get to be in the wedding?" Melissa asked.

"Yup."

"You are *so* lucky!" Melissa squealed.

"And Bob is really nice," Angela put in.

I pulled my knees up to my chest. "Bob is nice." I couldn't argue with that. "But..." Never mind. They wouldn't understand.

"You still wish you knew where your father was," Angela said.

"Yes," I said.

"Why don't you know where your father is?" Coral asked. Her parents were actually still married to each other. In her world, parents didn't get divorced. And dads didn't go years and years without seeing their kids.

"He left when my parents got divorced," I said. "My mom has no idea where he is. And neither does anyone else."

"Well, people don't just disappear," Coral said. "I bet you could find him if you tried."

"She's tried," Angela said in a tired voice. "Believe me, she's tried."

"I've tried everything—the internet, the library, all of our neighbors."

"She even tried a psychic!" Angela blurted out.

I glared at her. Had it ever occurred to Angela that maybe I didn't want people knowing about that?

"A *psychic?*" Melissa squealed. "Oooh! What was that like?"

I shrugged. "It was okay."

"What about a private detective?" Coral suggested.

"I can't afford a private detective," I said. "And even if I could, where would I find one who'd work for a thirteen-year-old?"

"Online?" Coral suggested. "I bet you could find someone really cheap online. And they'd never have to know you're only thirteen."

Hmm. "Maybe…"

"Yeah, but you have to be careful," Angela said. "There are a lot of scams online."

"Plus you'd probably need a credit card to pay for it," Melissa put in.

"I have a credit card," I said.

"You have a credit card?" Melissa raised an eyebrow.

"Well, sort of. My mom got me a debit card a few months ago and told me I could use it in an emergency."

"This isn't an emergency," Angela said.

It was as far as I was concerned. Okay, maybe it wasn't the kind of emergency my mom had in mind. But if that card would help me find my dad, I was willing to use it.

I turned to Coral. "Would you help me find a detective? One who isn't a scammer?"

"Sure," Coral said.

I hopped to my feet and picked up my towel.

Coral squinted at me. "Oh, you mean now?"

"Well…" We weren't really doing anything else.

"Don't you think you're getting a little carried away, Sam?" Angela asked. "How are you going to explain the charge to your mom?"

"I'll worry about that when the time comes," I said. "Come on. Let's go."

"Not me," Angela said, turning over on her towel. "Our moms talk, you know. If my mom finds out about this, I'll probably end up in just as much trouble as you."

I rolled my eyes. "I'm not going to get in trouble."

"Right," Angela said.

"I'll pass too," Melissa said, stretching out on her chair. "I need to tan at least twenty minutes on this side or I'll be uneven."

I turned to Coral. "I don't mind leaving," she said. "Let's go see if we can find you a detective."

Angela shook her head with disapproval. But I didn't see what the big deal was. My mom probably wouldn't even notice the charge. And if she did, I'd pay her back.

Coral and I gathered up our stuff, picked up our pool passes, and biked down the street to her house.

When we got there, we went up to Coral's bedroom and she opened her laptop. "This shouldn't be that hard. I'm pretty sure I've seen e-mails in my spam folder from people who say they can find anyone anywhere. Haven't you?"

I shrugged. "I don't ever check my spam folder."

I'd never been in Coral's bedroom before, so while she scanned her spam folder, I looked around. She had kind of a plain room. Green walls. Dark green comforter. And a poster that showed who-knew-how-many digits of pi. She was kind of a math geek.

"Here we go." Coral opened an e-mail that said *Find anyone, anywhere. Guaranteed!* in the subject header.

"Do you think that's a good one?"

"Let's check out his website." She double-clicked on the link and a website came up. "Whoa. He charges seventy-nine ninety-nine."

I just about choked. "That's a little much to put on my mom's debit card."

"I think we can do better than that," Coral said. She pulled up a search engine and typed in "find anyone." There were thousands of matches. But Coral went down the list, clicking from one website to another so fast she made my head spin.

Finally she stopped. "This one looks pretty good."

"Hey, they even tell you how they find people." I read the list out loud. "'Motor vehicle registration records, voter registration records, national telephone listings, property ownership records, consumer credit reporting agencies, magazine subscription databases, pilot licenses, and more.' Can we find out how much they charge?"

Coral scrolled to the bottom of the page. "Nineteen ninety-nine."

"That's not bad," I said, nodding.

"Should we go with this one?" Coral asked.

"Sure."

"Okay." Coral read from the form. "First we need your e-mail address."

"But my mom can read all my e-mail." I didn't know whether she *would* read it, but I didn't want to take any chances. I could just hear her if she suddenly came across an e-mail with my dad's address in it.

"I guess we can use my e-mail address and I'll let you know when I hear something," Coral offered. "My parents never check my e-mail."

"Okay." That worked for me.

"Now we need to type in what we know about your dad. The more information we can include, the better."

We filled in his name and we put my address in the blank for "former address."

"What about birthday?" Coral asked.

I shook my head. I didn't know when my dad's birthday was. "I know he's around thirty-three, though. My mom's thirty-two."

We counted back and figured out what year my dad had probably been born.

"Every little bit helps," Coral said, typing the information in. "Anything else?"

I squinted at the choices on the screen. I had no idea what city or state my dad lived in, what his Social Security number was, whether he practiced any religion, whether he was affiliated with any groups, or anything else. The only thing left to fill in was my credit card information.

I dug the card out of my wallet and read the numbers to Coral. Then she scrolled back over everything else we'd already typed in so we could double-check it. "Looks good. Should I click on 'Submit'?" Coral asked.

I bit my lip. There was still time to back out.

But I wasn't going to.

"Click on 'Submit,'" I said.

Now all I had to do was wait.

Chapter 8

That night I dreamed about Sarah again. This dream wasn't as vivid. In fact, I think I even knew I was dreaming, but I didn't want the dream to stop.

We were here in this house and we were playing hide-and-seek. I'm not sure how old we were. Older than three, but not as old as I am now.

"Come find me, Sam!" she called in a giggly voice.

I searched for her in the front closet…behind the living room couch…under the kitchen table. Finally, I found her in my mom's room, crouched behind a chair. She came out laughing. "Again, Sam! Again!"

So, we did it again. I pressed my forehead against our front door and counted. "One, two, three…" When I got to twenty, I went to look for her again. It went on like that several times, with her doing all the hiding and me doing all the seeking.

Then I said, "I want to hide this time."

Sarah tipped her head back. "Silly! You can't hide. Everyone knows where you are. But no one knows where I am."

And then I woke up.

No one knows where I am.

I opened my eyes and blinked a few times in the darkness. I rolled over and checked the clock on my phone. 2:14 AM. I groaned. I hugged my stuffed monkey to my chest and tried to go back to sleep, but I was wide awake.

I turned on my reading lamp, leaned over the edge of my bed and pulled out the book where I'd hidden the photo of Sarah and me. I slid the photo out and stared at it.

No one knows where I am.

Things always seem kind of creepy at night when you're alone in your room and everything's all dark, but I couldn't help but wonder whether my sister was somehow trying to communicate with me through my dreams. We were twins, after all. We had a connection to one another that other people didn't have.

I kept staring at the photo, looking for... I'm not sure what I was looking for, but whatever it was clearly wasn't there.

I lay back on my pillow and sighed. I tried to remember what it was like when Sarah was here. What it felt like to have a sister. But no matter how hard I strained my brain, all I could remember were tiny bits and pieces: a little glass bird that hung in the window and spun around...a humming noise in the bedroom like a fan or a humidifier...somebody throwing up—was that me? Or Sarah?

I also remembered high-heeled shoes clicking on the kitchen floor and a dog barking and my mom yelling and a little kid crying...but nothing came together to form a real scene that made any sense. The memories were there, though. Memories of what it was like when we were a family. I could feel them hanging there in the air, just beyond my fingertips. But I couldn't grab any of them. And the harder I tried, the heavier my eyelids grew.

At some point, I must have fallen asleep, because the next time I opened my eyes my bedroom was bright with sunlight. It didn't even feel like I'd slept, but obviously I had. I sat up and rubbed my eyes.

It was nine o'clock. My mom was at work. Which meant Sherlock and I had the house to ourselves. I got up and went about my morning routine, but I felt off balance somehow, like something was out of place.

Maybe it was that bump on my forehead. I lifted my bangs and peered at myself in the mirror. The purplish bump was still there, but it looked better. The swelling had gone down some.

No, it wasn't the bump that was bothering me. It was this sort of sixth-sense feeling that my sister was still alive. That she was out there somewhere, searching for me. Maybe it was a twin thing. I felt it in the middle of the night when everything was shadowy and unreal. But I also felt it now. In the light of day.

It was *real.*

I already knew what my mom would say if I told her that. She'd say "There's no such thing as a sixth sense. Sarah is dead. It's time to move on." But would my dad see it the same way? After all, he was there when the canoe tipped over. His opinion would carry more weight than my mom's. If this detective that Coral found online actually found my dad, I could talk to him about all of this. Who knows? Maybe he'd even help me look for Sarah.

Which made me wonder…had Coral gotten an answer from that guy yet? I decided to text her and find out.

It took her a little while to respond. **Hold on, let me check. I just woke up, so I haven't checked my e-mail yet.**

I waited while she checked her e-mail.

Doesn't look like it, she texted again after a little bit. **But we just filled out that form yesterday, you know. It could take a few days to hear back.**

Yeah, I guess. Thanks for checking.

A very long day stretched out ahead of me. I had no idea what I was going to do with myself. I could bring some boxes up to my room and start packing. But I didn't feel like doing that.

I hadn't practiced my flute in a couple days. I snapped open my flute case and twisted the three sections together. But once it was together, I didn't feel like practicing either. Finally, I got out my bike.

I don't know whether this was something I decided to do or whether my bike was somehow on autopilot. But I got on it and started pedaling. Before I knew it, I found myself heading down Sixth Street, which took me to Rockford Road, which eventually became a gravel road. Old Quarry Road.

I couldn't remember the last time I'd been out this way. Maybe I hadn't ever been out here. I doubt my mom ever came out here. Who else would have brought me?

It was a really quiet road. There were no houses along the way. No cars or other people out on bikes. No animals. Not even any wind through the trees. The only sound was my bike tires crunching the gravel.

I had a feeling I shouldn't be out here. At least not by myself. There wasn't a single person in the whole world who knew where I was. What if I got kidnapped? Or murdered? What if my murderer dumped my body in the quarry and nobody ever found it?

I swallowed hard. My imagination was going crazy. This was Clearwater, Iowa. We didn't have murderers here. But wasn't that what people always said whenever there was a murder in their small town?

The gravel road ended at a small parking area, but there were no cars in the lot. I could sort of see the quarry through the trees. I could smell it too. It smelled like rotting weeds.

I got off my bike and wheeled it up the narrow dirt path. A mosquito buzzed by my ear. I swatted it away.

I kept going until the trees ended and I came to a chain-link fence. I wondered how long this fence had been here. Was it here when my dad brought Sarah out here?

I could see the trees on the other side of the quarry, but I couldn't see down into the pit. I had to get closer. I leaned my bike against a tree, then slowly walked toward to the fence. It wasn't very high. I stuck my toe in one of the gaps and curled my fingers around the bar along the top of the fence. Then I heaved myself up onto the top of the fence and jumped down to the other side, landing on my hands and knees. I quickly picked myself up and dusted myself off.

This was it. There were just a few feet of tall grass and rock, then the ground just sort of dropped off and the quarry lay down below. A huge mouth of water, ready to swallow me up if I stepped over the edge.

I took a couple of steps back and grabbed for the fence. Then I gazed down at the water again. It was a long way down. Too far to launch a canoe from. So where had my dad put his canoe in?

It was several miles around the whole quarry. He could've done it anywhere. Anywhere but here.

I started walking beside the fence. Every now and then I stopped to scratch my ankles. I hoped it was just the tall grass that was making me itch and not bugs. As I walked, the patch of grass grew wider and wider. Holding on to the fence for support, I carefully made my way down a steep hill. When I got to the bottom, I found myself standing in a small clearing.

It wasn't so far down to the water here. Maybe a foot or two. I had no idea how deep the water was. People say the quarry is 300 feet deep, but not here at the edge. You probably could get a canoe in here.

I looked around for a long branch. Something I could put in the water to get an idea of how deep it really was. I spotted one over by a sign that read "Danger! Absolutely No Swimming, Boating, or Canoeing." I ran over and picked up the branch.

It was about two inches around and stood as tall as my chest. I took it over to the edge of the water and slowly lowered it down. Down, down, down until only the tip where I held it remained out of the water. The other end still hadn't touched bottom. I let the branch go and it bobbed to the surface, then floated out of reach.

I shivered. The water was really murky, just like my mom said. It was so thick and cloudy it didn't wave or ripple or anything. It just sat there, unmoving. Dead.

I could see why Sarah's body was never found. Even with all the fancy equipment the police must use to search for people in the water, it would be impossible to find someone here. You'd never even see your hand in front of you.

But despite all that, standing here right now, gazing out over the water, that sixth sense was just as strong as it had been back at my house. Maybe even stronger.

I knew my sister wasn't down there.

* * *

"Are you out of your mind?" Angela asked when we video chatted again later that afternoon.

I couldn't just keep carrying all this around in my head. I had to talk to someone. Obviously I couldn't talk to my mom. I'd never been able to talk to my Grandma Sperling. We didn't see each other enough to have that kind of relationship. If things were different, I might have been able to talk to Bob's mother. If I'd been born into her family, I mean. But the only reason she and I were anything at all to each other was because my mom was marrying her son. Really, the only person I could talk to was Angela.

"I'll say it one more time. There is no way your sister could still be alive," Angela said, putting her face right up to her screen. "You do know that, don't you?"

I didn't answer.

"Your sister is dead, Sam," Angela went on. "She's been dead for ten years." She sounded just like my mother.

"Gee, tell me what you really think," I muttered.

"Do you want me to?" Angela asked seriously.

I shrugged. It didn't matter. Angela always told me what she really thought.

"Well, I think you don't want your mom and Bob to get married."

My mouth dropped open. "That's not true!" I didn't want Bob to adopt me, but I didn't care whether they got married or not.

"I think it is," Angela said. "But you can't tell your mom that, so you're putting all this energy into other stuff. Like looking for your dad. And wondering whether your sister could still be alive. It's, like, some kind of distraction. Because you can't deal with the truth."

No! Angela was wrong. Way wrong.

"If you really want to know what I think, here it is. I think you should quit digging around in the past and concentrate on the future. Bob's nice. Why don't you give him a chance?"

"Yeah, well maybe you should give your real dad a chance too," I grumbled.

Angela clammed up when I said that. In all the years we'd been friends, I don't think we'd ever had a real fight. But I could tell we were on the verge of one right now.

"You don't know anything about my father, Sam," Angela said coolly.

"And you don't know anything about mine. You don't know anything about my sister, either."

At first Angela didn't say anything. Then in a small voice she said, "Okay, maybe neither one of us should tell the other what to do."

"Maybe not," I agreed, relieved we weren't going to fight about it.

But nothing had really been solved.

Chapter 9

After dinner my phone buzzed. Coral wanted to Face-Time!

My mom and Bob were over at our new house checking out the new countertops that were put in today, so I didn't have to worry about them walking in on me. I answered right away.

"I thought you'd like to know we heard back from that detective guy," Coral said.

"Yeah?" I elbowed my bedroom door closed just in case my mom and Bob came home early, then crawled up onto my bed with my phone.

"Don't get too excited. I don't have a single, definite address and phone number for you," Coral said from her desk. "What I have is three addresses and phone numbers. The e-mail says they're pretty sure one of these Joseph Wrights is the one you're searching for. But if it turns out none of them is, they'll keep looking for free."

"Okay," I said, pulling my legs up under me. My whole body trembled. "So what have you got?" Finally, I was about to get some *real* information!

"Do you have something to write with?" Coral asked.

"Yeah." I reached over and grabbed a pencil from my desk and a piece of scratch paper from my garbage can. My hand was shaking so hard I could barely write. But somehow I managed to copy the names, addresses, and phone numbers as Coral read them off. There was one Joseph Wright in San Diego, California, another in Richland, Minnesota, and a third in Omaha, Nebraska.

"Thanks, Coral," I said. "Thanks for everything."

"No problem. Good luck, Sam. I hope you find what you're looking for."

At first, I just sat there on my bed, my phone in my hand, staring at those names, addresses, and phone numbers. *One of these men was probably my dad.*

Was it possible for a thirteen-year-old to have a heart attack? All I had to do was pick the right number and I could be talking to my dad in about twenty seconds. Even if I didn't pick the right number, there were only two others to try. Five minutes, tops, and I'd know which of those Joseph Wrights was my dad. Assuming one of them was.

With my mom out of the house, this was the perfect time to call. Oh, my gosh! I'd never been so nervous in my entire life. How was I supposed to make a phone call when I literally could not breathe?

Should I call or text? Or FaceTime?

I could also just write them each a letter. I had their addresses too. There were two reasons a letter might be better. One, I wouldn't have to explain the charge on the phone bill later (though I still might have to explain the charge for hiring the detective who got me the addresses and phone numbers). And two, I could take my time and figure out exactly what I wanted to say. But I might have to wait to hear back. And what if the real Joseph Wright never replied? No, calling was definitely the better choice. That way I'd get answers right away. And I'd get to hear my dad's voice, but I wouldn't have to see his face if he wasn't happy to hear from me.

I wished I had more than just names, addresses, and phone numbers. I wished I had photographs. And basic information like whether these guys were married or had children. I'd never thought about my dad having a whole new family before. But he could. Angela's dad did.

"Just do it!" I said out loud. "Pick a number and call."

But what was I supposed to say? I argued with myself. "Hi, this is Sam, your long-lost daughter?" What if all he had to say back was "Yeah, so?" Maybe calling was just as bad as FaceTiming.

I remembered what Angela said about how when you don't know your dad, you can pretend he's anyone you want him to be. Maybe she was right. Maybe deep down I did just want to pretend. Maybe I didn't want to find out who he really was.

No, I wanted to know him. I wanted to know whether he ever thought about me. Whether he ever thought about Sarah. And the only way I was ever going to find out anything was to call.

So...which Joseph Wright should I try first?

Probably the one in San Diego. I knew my dad had been in San Diego seven years ago when he sent me that postcard, so San Diego was a good place to start.

I crept out into the hallway and listened for my mom and Bob. It didn't sound like they were back yet. But if I didn't hurry this up, they would be. I tiptoed back to my room, closed the door, and hopped back up onto my bed. Then I took a deep breath and quickly tapped in the San Diego number before I could change my mind. The phone felt slippery in my fingers. I could feel my heart in my throat. I almost hung up, but I forced myself to hang on until someone finally picked up on the fifth ring.

"Hello?" It was a woman. A woman around my mom's age, it sounded like. My dad's new wife?

"Um, hi," I said. My mind suddenly went blank. Why didn't I at least write out a speech ahead of time?

"Yes?" the woman said.

I swallowed hard, then plunged ahead. "Um, you don't know me. My name is Sam. Sam *Wright.*"

"Yes?" The woman sounded a little impatient now.

My heart was pounding so hard I thought my chest would crack open. "D-d-does that name mean anything to you?" I asked.

"Well, other than the fact we share the same last name, no." The woman sounded nicer this time. "Should it?"

"I don't know," I said. And then it hit me: if this woman was my dad's new wife, this call could come as a huge shock.

"I-I-I'm looking for my father," I stammered. "His name is Joseph Wright. I know there's a Joseph Wright at this number. C-could I maybe talk to him, please?"

"I'm afraid not," the woman replied matter-of-factly. "Joseph died three years ago."

"What?" No!

"He couldn't have been your father, though," the woman went on.

I breathed a sigh of relief when she said that. This was the wrong Joseph Wright. My dad was still alive.

But the feeling disappeared almost as quickly as it had appeared. "How do you know?" I asked. Wasn't it possible my dad ran off to California after Sarah died, got married, and never told his new wife about me?

"Joseph and I were married for fifteen years. We both wanted children very much, but Joseph..." she broke off.

"What?"

"He couldn't have children," she said softly.

"Oh." I suddenly felt very sorry. Not to mention embarrassed. That was such personal information. And it was none of my business.

I felt bad for this woman. She seemed so nice. I bet her husband, Joseph, was nice too. He probably would've been a good dad if he had had children.

"Well, thanks anyway," I said, not knowing what else to say. "And—I'm really sorry about your husband." Then I hung up.

Okay. One down, two to go. After making one call, it wasn't quite as hard to do it again. I wiped my slippery hands on my shorts, then tried the next Joseph on my list. The one in Minnesota.

This time my call went to voice mail.

Goosebumps dotted my arms.

I knew that voice!

I couldn't believe that after all those years, I recognized my dad's voice. But I did. "Yo." *Yo, Sammy! Yo, Sarah! Yo, Suzanne!* He always said yo instead of hello. "We can't come to the phone right now, so leave a message. We'll get back to you." *Beep!*

I slammed my phone down.

I could feel the blood pounding inside my head. My hands were shaking. *It was him.* I knew it was him.

I took a deep breath and tried to calm down.

Another breath.

And another.

What was I going to do now?

I got up from my bed and wandered around my room. He was married. Or at least living with someone. The voice said, *"We'll get back to you."*

I grabbed my pillow, then set it back down. I looked out the window, but my eyes didn't focus. I replayed that voice, *his* voice, over and over inside my head. *Yo. We can't come to the phone right now, so leave a message. We'll get back to you.*

He was in Minnesota. Just one state away. Like Angela's dad. Had he been there all this time? Why hadn't he at least called me once in the last however many years? *Why?*

I had to call him back. I had to call him back right now and leave him a message. I picked up the phone and started dialing before I could chicken out.

This time the voice mail picked up on the second ring.

"Yo. We can't come to the phone right now, so leave a message. We'll get back to you."

"Hello? Dad?...It's me, Sam..." My throat tightened as my eyes filled with tears. "Do you remember me? Please call me," I said. I barely managed to get my phone number out before the tears started to roll down my cheeks.

Chapter 10

I didn't set my phone down the rest of the night. *Come on, Dad. Hurry up and call me back before Mom gets home!*

My phone stayed silent.

While I waited, I texted Angela: **You're never going to believe what happened.** I told her everything.

But Angela just couldn't get excited for me. **How do you know that guy is really your dad?** she texted back.

I recognized his voice.

You recognized his voice? She was probably rolling her eyes at me. **Sam, it's only been five months since I talked to my father and I hardly recognized his voice.**

You're kidding! Even for Angela, that sounded extreme.

Why would I recognize a voice I hardly ever hear?

Because he's your dad.

Father, Angela corrected.

Whatever. I didn't want to argue over words. The point is there's a connection between you. A father-daughter connection. You'll always recognize your dad's voice because of that connection.

I don't know. I don't think so, Angela argued. Look, Sam. I don't know whether this guy is your dad or not. But just because you're father and daughter doesn't mean you're always connected. Sometimes connections get broken.

Maybe. But that didn't mean they had to stay broken.

It was almost ten o'clock when Angela and I stopped texting. I knew my mom would be home soon. I would've thought that wherever my dad was, he'd be getting home soon too. I imagined a man with white-blond hair, walking through his house, picking up his phone when he realized he had voice mail. I imagined the look of surprise on his face when he heard my voice, because of course he'd recognize my voice too. Maybe he'd replay that message over and over again just to hear my voice. He could be checking a clock on the wall right that very second, wondering whether it was too late to call me back.

It's not. I tried to send thought waves through the phone line. *Call me. Please call me.*

He never called that night.

Or the next day.

Or the day after that.

And there were a million reasons why he wouldn't have called. Reasons other than he just didn't want to talk to me. One, he could have been on vacation. Two, he could have been working a lot. Three, maybe he worked nights and slept during the day. That would make it awfully hard to find a good time to call me back.

Right?

It was also possible he had a new wife who had gotten the message and erased it before he'd even heard it. Even if he was perfectly happy to hear from me, a new wife might not be so happy about it. Now that I really thought about it, I probably shouldn't have left a message like that.

Or maybe there was another reason. Maybe he was afraid my mom would answer the phone.

After three days, I figured it was okay to try him again. But what if he really didn't want to talk to me? What if he didn't care about me at all? I wasn't ready to deal with that possibility, so I decided to hold off a couple more days. We were coming up on the weekend. Surely he'd call during the weekend.

But on Saturday Mom had a huge list of things she wanted to do. First she wanted to pick up the wedding invitations. Then she wanted to stop in at the bakery, the florist, and Xavier's, the place where she and Bob were having the wedding reception, just to make sure everything was set. She also had an appointment at Julianne's for her final dress fitting and then she was hoping to meet with the minister to make her final music selections. Bob's mother was coming too. They had the whole day planned out, and my mom insisted on dragging me along for all of it.

I hesitated. "I don't know." I was sure my dad was going to call that day and I didn't want to miss him. Sure, I'd have my phone with me, but I couldn't exactly talk to him in front of my mom.

Mom looked hurt. "Sam, taking care of these last-minute wedding details is supposed to be fun. I would've thought you'd want to come along."

"Fine," I said with a heavy sigh. "I'll go." It wasn't like I had a choice anyway. So, when my mom wasn't looking, I set my phone to vibrate and shoved it in my shorts pocket. At least I'd know whether my dad called or not. Then she and I headed out.

We stopped to pick up Bob's mother first. "I'm so glad you girls invited me along!" she said as she climbed into the front seat. "We're going to have such a nice day."

Yeah, real nice.

Then the two of them started talking about how close the wedding was and how it was finally going to happen. I just sat in the back with my hand resting on my phone and watched the world go by.

We stopped at the florist first. Everything was in order there. Then we stopped at the bakery. Everything was in order there too. On the way to the stationery store, my mom said, "They were supposed to tile the bathrooms at the new house yesterday. It's not that far out of the way. Would anyone like to go over and see it?" She glanced pointedly at me in the rearview mirror.

"Oh, I would love to see your new place," Bob's mother said. "I've been by it, you know. But I've never been inside."

"You haven't?" Mom sounded surprised.

"No."

"Well, then we're definitely going to stop." Mom put on her turn signal, moved into the left lane, and turned onto Ridge Drive. "It's been a while since you've seen the house too, Sam. It's almost done."

"Great," I said, trying to sound enthusiastic.

"This is such a nice neighborhood," Bob's mom prattled on as we drove past rows of identical two-story beige houses. "Dan and Becky really like it." I couldn't remember whether Dan was Bob's brother or Becky was his sister. Either way, they lived about two blocks from where we were going to live, which my mom considered a huge bonus.

"I'm sure we'll be very happy here," Mom said. "Don't you think so, Sam?"

I gave the correct answer, which was "Yes, of course." After all, my mom and Bob were plunking down a huge amount of money for this house. And most of my friends lived nearby. As far as my mom was concerned, there was absolutely no reason I shouldn't be happy here. So, of course, I would be.

Mom pulled up in front of a house that looked like all the other half-finished houses on the block. I don't know how she knew which one was ours. There was no grass and no driveway yet. But there were doors on the house now. A front door and probably a garage door too. Though it was hard to tell for sure because the garage door was up and there was somebody sawing something in the garage.

We all got out of the car and the guy in the garage stopped whatever he was doing. It turned out he was the builder, so he was thrilled to show us around.

Bob's mother had nice things to say about every-thing—the new cabinets and hardwood floor in the kitchen, the screen porch that wasn't screened in yet, the fireplace in the living room, the ceramic tile in the entry-way. The carpet wasn't in yet in the living room and din-ing room, but the builder said it was coming in the next couple of days.

He led us up the uncarpeted stairway so we could check out the bedrooms and the freshly tiled bathrooms. My bedroom was the first one at the top of the stairs. There was a guy working on the window seat in there. He had sawdust in his hair, on his face, and all over his shirt. He looked up when he saw me lingering in the doorway.

My mom and Bob's mom continued down the hall with the builder.

"Are you the lucky lady who gets this room?" Saw-dust Man asked with a wide grin that showed the gap between his two top front teeth.

"Yup." That was me. The lucky lady.

It was a nice room. I loved the built-in bookshelves. And I couldn't complain about the view of the woods from the window. But nice as it was, it just didn't feel like my room. And the rest of the house didn't feel like my house. It didn't feel like anybody's house. It had no personality. No feelings. No memories.

The thing about houses is they're filled with the mem-ories of all the people who have ever lived in them. Our little house on Hartman Lane has memories of me, my mom, my dad, Sarah, and lots of people I've never even met. Those memories are all part of that house. When we move, my mom and I will remember things that happened when we lived there. But in a way, I think memories stay with a house. Like ghosts.

I knew exactly what my mom would say to that. She'd say, "Well, I guess we'll just have to create memories for our new house as soon as we can. And there are no such things as ghosts."

The only problem is, this is a huge house. It would take a long time to create enough memories to fill the whole thing. Honestly, I wasn't sure I was up to it.

* * *

It had been five days since I'd left the message on my dad's answering machine and he still hadn't called me back. *What is the deal?* I wondered as I paced anxiously back and forth in my room.

Was his voice mail broken? Maybe he got the message, wrote my number down so he could call me back later, then lost the number? Maybe he'd been tearing his whole house apart like a crazy person, trying to find my number, scared to death he'll never hear from me again.

Or maybe I was wrong? Maybe the person I called wasn't my dad after all?

No. One thing I was sure of—that was my dad's voice on the recording.

It couldn't be that he just didn't want to talk to me. That he just didn't care. I remembered stuff he used to do, like monkey back rides and monkey faces. He was the monkey man and I was his Sammy Bear. He had to call me back. He just *had* to.

Maybe he was in the hospital? Or maybe he'd been in a terrible accident? What if after all these years I finally found my dad, only to have him die some terrible death before I could make contact with him? Like the Joseph Wright in San Diego did?

Maybe I should call that number again and leave another message? This was a good time to do it—Mom and Bob were busy addressing wedding invitations. They weren't likely to check on me for a while.

I could say something like, "Hey, even if you don't ever want to see me or talk to me again, at least call me back and tell me. Just so I know."

I reached under my mattress and pulled out the scrap of paper with the information about the three Joseph Wrights. I didn't really need the paper, though. I had his phone number memorized.

My heart pounding, I picked up my phone and punched in the number. This time his phone didn't ring at all. Instead I got a bunch of tones and a recording that said, "We're sorry. The number you have dialed has been disconnected."

Disconnected? I stared at the phone in my hand. That couldn't be right. I'd just dialed that number five days ago. Maybe my finger slipped and I dialed the wrong number?

I tried again. But all I got was the same recording.

Chapter 11

It wasn't fair. I'd tried so hard to find him. And just when I'd gotten close, he slipped away.

Well, I knew where my dad was five days ago. Maybe I could call Information and find out where he went? Maybe there was a forwarding number? I dialed 411.

The operator who answered told me she had listings for two Joseph Wrights and one D. Wright in Richland, Minnesota. I knew I needed the Joseph Wright who lived at 7430 Sheridan Avenue South in Richland, Minnesota. But the lady just said that that number was disconnected and there was no further information.

Argh! "Thanks anyway," I said, hanging up.

I didn't know what else to do, so I FaceTimed with Angela to see if she had any advice.

"Drop it," she said right away. "That's my advice."

"I can't!" I flopped back onto my bed.

"Well, if this guy really is your dad, obviously he's trying to tell you that he doesn't want to talk to you. I'm sorry, Sam, but some fathers are like that. They walk out and then they pretend that whole part of their lives when they were married to your mom never happened. Even if they had kids. They just cut the kids out of their lives too. Like they don't even care."

Maybe Angela's father was like that, but I never thought mine could be like that too. I rolled to my side and picked at a loose thread on my comforter. "He sent me a postcard when I was six. He cared about me then. What changed since then?"

Angela's voice softened. "See, this is what I was trying to tell you a couple of weeks ago. Back then you could still pretend your dad was a good guy and he loved you and you could tell yourself there were all these good reasons why he hasn't been in your life—" I could tell by the tone of Angela's voice that she was trying to be nice, but her words cut me to the core.

"Now you have to face the truth about him," Angela went on. "And you don't even know the truth. The truth could actually be worse than you're imagining. Your father could be some sort of criminal or something. He could be a drug dealer or a kidnapper or—"

A kidnapper?

"Oh no!" I cried as a new idea took shape in my head. I sat up on my bed.

"I know. It's terrible to think of your own father that way, but—"

"No! Listen to me, Angela," I interrupted. "What if he *is* a kidnapper? What if he…kidnapped my sister?"

Angela let out a short laugh, then cut it off when she realized I was serious.

"That would explain it," I said. "It would explain everything: why I have this feeling she's still alive, why he hasn't been in touch all these years, why his phone was suddenly disconnected—"

Whoa! What was I saying? That my dad...what? Faked Sarah's death, then took her away? Was that what I really thought? That my dad was the kind of person who would do such a thing?

It was possible. If he really wanted to hurt my mom. Grandma Sperling said my mom and dad never had a good marriage.

Plus Sarah's body was never found. I haven't heard from my dad since I was six years old, and even then I didn't actually see him. I only got a postcard. If my dad had my sister with him (the sister everyone thinks is dead), and then I called him up out of the blue, no way would he call me back. He wouldn't want me to know about Sarah.

"Sam, your father did not kidnap your sister. She drowned in the old quarry ten years ago."

"No, she didn't," I argued. I was nearly one hundred per cent sure of that.

"Sam!"

I could tell Angela thought I'd totally lost my mind, but I didn't care. I needed a plan. I needed to figure out what I was going to do next.

"Angela, do you know where Richland, Minnesota, is?"

"I think it's one of the suburbs near Minneapolis. Why?"

"How far is that from your dad's?"

"I don't know," Angela said warily. "An hour to an hour and a half—"

Angela was going to Minnesota *tomorrow.* "I've got to go to Minnesota with you," I said. "Can I?" If I could get as far as Hill Valley with Angela, maybe once I was there I could figure out how to get the rest of the way to Richland.

"What?" Angela cried.

I took a deep breath. "I need to go to 7430 Sheridan Avenue South in Richland and meet this Joseph Wright and find out why his phone is disconnected."

But I knew that if I was right about all this, if this Joseph Wright was my dad, and if he really did fake my sister's death and kidnap her all those years ago, he probably didn't just disconnect his phone. He probably took Sarah and ran.

"Sam, you're scaring me," Angela said. "This is just too crazy...."

Still, I could go to 7430 Sheridan Avenue South and find out whether anyone was living there. Even if no one was, I could go to the neighbors and find out whether the man who had lived there had a young girl with him. Maybe I could even get a clue to where they went.

"Please, Angela," I begged. "I need to go to Minnesota with you!"

"I don't know, Sam," Angela said. "If you really

think this is what happened, I think you need to tell your mom—"

"She won't believe me!" She was too wrapped up in wedding plans to even listen to me. *You and I are closing the door on this chapter of our lives. It's time to look forward and put the past behind us.*

"Well, then maybe you could talk to Bob?" Angela suggested. "He's a policeman. Maybe he could—"

"I'm definitely not talking to Bob! Not about this. Come on, Angela. Please?" I pleaded. "If I can get to Hill Valley, I can maybe take a bus to Richland. Then I can go over to that house and see what I can find out. It is possible I'm wrong about all this, you know—" I didn't think so, but I knew Angela was more likely to give in if I said it.

"If I'm wrong, I'll just come back to Clearwater with you and pretend it never happened," I promised. "But if I'm right, don't you think I have a right to know?"

Angela didn't say anything right away. Was she starting to come around?

"I'd be with you in Hill Valley most of the time," I went on. "We'd have fun. You could show me around and we could...well, I don't know what there is to do in Hill Valley."

"Not much," Angela grumbled. "But now that you mention it, it might be nice to have you there at my father's. Especially if things don't go well."

Yes!

"I'll text him and see whether he'll let me bring a friend, okay?"

94

"Okay!" I squealed. "Thanks, Angela. Thank you so much."

"Don't thank me yet," she said as she picked up her phone. "He might say no."

I could hear Angela's mom calling her in the distance. She turned toward the voice, then back to me. "I better go," she said to me. "I'll text you when I hear from him, okay? It could be a while. He never texts back right away."

"Okay. Bye."

I was practically bouncing off the walls waiting for her to text me back. Oh my gosh! What if Sarah really was alive and living with my dad? The thought gave me goosebumps.

But then I thought of something else. If my dad did kidnap my sister, why did he just take *her?* Why didn't he take me too?

I didn't have an answer for that. But there was one thing I did know. The voice I heard on the phone was definitely my dad's. That was why I had to go to Richland, Minnesota.

Come on, Mr. Hunter. Please say yes!

Of course, I still needed to clear it with my mom. So I pulled myself together. I took several deep breaths and ran my fingers through my hair. Then I calmly went to see how she and Bob were coming on the wedding invitations.

I was surprised to find her alone. But there she was, reading a magazine on the couch in the family room. Sherlock was sound asleep in her lap. Except for the stack of stamped wedding invitations piled on the coffee table, it was just like how things were a year ago. Before she and Bob got engaged and started spending every waking minute together.

"Where's Bob?" I asked.

She looked up and smiled. "He's got an early meeting in the morning, so he went home."

"Oh." I perched on the edge of the couch. "Angela's going to visit her dad tomorrow."

"Yes, I know." Mom set her magazine aside. "I talked to Anne today. I understand Angela's not very happy about this trip."

"No, she's not," I agreed. "She doesn't like her dad very much." I grabbed one of Mom's Health magazines from the coffee table.

"Actually, she invited me to go with her," I said casually. "It's okay, isn't it? She could use some moral support."

"Moral support?" Mom cocked her head at me as though wondering what I was trying to get away with now.

"Yeah." I shrugged like my going with Angela was no big deal. But inside my heart was hammering. It was the biggest deal in the world!

"It's only six days. I'll be back next Sunday night." If I acted like it wasn't a big deal, maybe she would too.

"You can't go, Sam," Mom said quietly but firmly.

"What?" I sat up. "Why not?"

Mom looked surprised that I would even ask. "My bridal shower is on Saturday."

Crud! I'd forgotten all about that.

"This is important, Mom," I said in as reasonable a voice as I could muster. "I really have to go with Angela. She'll be totally miserable if I don't."

Sherlock raised his head and glanced from one of us to the other, then hopped down and scampered away.

Mom shifted her position so her whole body was facing me. "Bob's mother and all his sisters and sisters-in-law have been planning this shower for months," she explained. "They've worked very hard. How would it look if my own daughter didn't show up?"

"Who cares how it looks!" I shouted, leaping to my feet. I slammed the magazine down on the coffee table and accidentally knocked a few of the wedding invitations to the floor. "You're always so concerned about what Bob's family thinks!"

Her face tight, Mom leaned over to pick up the invitations. She didn't even respond to what I said. All she said was, "I'm sorry, Sam. But the answer is no."

I felt a pain in my chest. I was too old for a temper tantrum, but tears stung my eyes. How could she say no?

"It's not fair!" I said, even though I knew that argument never worked with her.

She shot me a warning look.

"It's *your* shower, not mine. And it's just one day. I can't believe you'd say no because of one day. Angela *needs* me, Mom!" I pleaded.

But Mom wasn't buying it. "I need you too," she said in a small voice.

"No, you don't," I muttered. "All you need is Bob and his mother and the rest of his stupid family." With that, I stormed up to my bedroom.

I half expected her to follow me and tell me I was wrong, but she didn't. And the fact that she didn't made me even madder.

I was really fuming when my phone buzzed a few minutes later. **He said yes,** Angela texted.

He did? I texted back.

Yeah. Did you ask your mom? Did she say it was okay too?

I talked to her. Then words flew from my thumbs before I could stop them. **She said it's okay. You guys can pick me up whenever you're ready tomorrow.**

Chapter 12

I'd never done anything like this before. Sure, I'd told a few little white lies now and then. Hasn't everyone? But I'd never gone ahead and done something my mom specifically said I couldn't do. Of course, she'd never said I couldn't do something this important before, either. My entire life hinged on this trip to Minnesota.

I set my alarm for 7:00 AM, the time my mom usually left for work, but I was wide awake at 6:30. I wondered whether I'd see things differently after a good night's sleep, whether I'd change my mind about going. But I was just as determined to go today as I'd been last night.

For half an hour, I lay in bed scratching Sherlock's chin and listening to my mom move around the house getting ready for work. I felt a little bit guilty, knowing what I was about to do (Boy, was she going to mad when she got home and found me gone!), but not guilty enough to change my mind. Eventually she'd understand why I had to do this. Maybe she'd even thank me one day. If I actually found Sarah as well as my dad.

At 6:45 I heard my bedroom door open. I closed my eyes and pretended I was asleep until I heard my door latch shut again. I don't think I even breathed until I heard the garage door going up and the car starting.

As soon as I heard the garage door coming back down, I rolled over and switched my alarm off. Then I threw off my covers and leaped to my window. I stuck my finger between two slats of mini blinds and watched my mom back down the driveway. By the time she got home this afternoon, I'd already be in Minnesota.

I let the blinds drop back into place and raced to my closet. I hadn't dared to pack anything last night, just in case my mom walked in. But now I hauled my suitcase down from the shelf in my closet and filled it with clothes, makeup, hair dryer, flat iron and a couple of books. I put on a pair of shorts and a T-shirt, then quickly ran a comb through my hair. I started to leave, but then went back to grab the photo of me and Sarah from under my bed.

Finally, I went to the kitchen to write Mom a note.

> Dear Mom,
>   I'm sorry, but I had to do this. I had to go with Angela. I know you'll be mad, but I had to do it anyway. I'll explain why when I get back.
>   Love, Sam
> P.S. I hope your shower is nice.

I grabbed my phone and popped it into my purse. As I did, I realized that probably the first thing Mom would do when she read my note was call my phone and ream me out. So, I picked up my phone, powered it all the way off, then dropped it back into my purse.

Would Mom call Angela's dad's house next? I doubted she knew the number, but she could probably get it easily enough from Angela's mom. Well, there wasn't much I could do about that. Fortunately, it was too far of a trip for her to just drive up there and drag me home by my ear. I was pretty sure that if I managed to get there, she'd have to let me stay the whole week. And while I was there, I'd find a way to get myself to Richland.

I double-checked my suitcase to make sure I had everything. Then I went to the front door to wait for Angela and her brother.

At exactly seven minutes past eight they pulled into the driveway. Andrew was driving a red Honda Civic, which he'd bought earlier that summer. I hadn't seen much of Andrew lately, but let me tell you, he was looking mighty fine when he stepped out of his car. He'd been working in the lumberyard at Menards all summer to pay for the Honda Civic, and lifting all those heavy planks of wood had done beautiful things to his arms. I really regretted not taking a little more time with my hair that morning.

"Hey, Sam," he said as he popped the trunk. My knees turned to jelly when he grabbed my suitcase and tossed it in the trunk with the others, but somehow I managed to get myself into the backseat with Angela.

"I'm glad you talked me into this," Angela said, moving her purse over to make room for me. "It'll be a lot easier to handle my dad if you're there too."

I squeezed her hand. I was glad she was happy to have me along. "Everything will be fine," I told her. "You'll see."

"Ready to roll, ladies?" Andrew eyed us through the rearview mirror. I loved how he called us "ladies."

I buckled my seat belt. "Ready," I said.

As Andrew backed down the driveway, I leaned over and whispered to Angela, "I can't believe your mom's letting him drive all the way to Minnesota!" He wasn't even eighteen yet.

In fact, if my mom had originally said I could go, but then found out Andrew was driving, she probably would've changed her mind.

Angela shrugged. "My mom didn't want to drive us. She doesn't want to see my dad or his new wife. And Andrew really wanted a car up there. That's about all he cares about these days. He didn't care whether we went or not, as long as he got to have his car. So letting him drive seemed like a good solution all around. Besides, it's mostly interstate between here and Hill Valley and there isn't a lot of traffic."

Andrew turned onto Interstate 380 and cranked up the music. I realized I'd never left town without an adult before. I felt all grown-up and mature…and excited…and scared…

It wasn't too late to ask Andrew to turn around and take me back home. If I went home right now, my mom would never know that I almost snuck off to Minnesota.

But I had to go. I had to find out the truth about my family. So, I sat back against my seat and settled in for the long ride.

Angela and I watched some videos on her phone. Then she opened a new game. "Have you seen this?" she asked. "It's called Zombie Marbles."

I watched her play a little bit. It looked fun.

"You should download it. Then we can play against each other," Angela said.

I would download it. But not now. I didn't want to turn my phone on. "I think I'll just read," I said, reaching into my purse for a book.

We stopped for lunch at a Pizza Hut somewhere in northern Iowa. They had a buffet. But before we got food, Angela and I went to comb our hair and use the bathroom. When we came out, I skidded to a stop. There was a lady dressed in a nurse's outfit standing at the cash register. From the back, she looked just like my mom.

"What's the matter?" Angela asked.

"My mom—" I began. When the woman turned around, I breathed a sigh of relief.

"What about your mom?" Angela asked, glancing from me to the woman and back again.

"Nothing," I said, hurrying back to our table.

Angela grabbed my arm. "What do you mean nothing?" She narrowed her eyes at me. "Your mom knows you came with me, doesn't she?"

I didn't answer.

"Doesn't she?" Angela repeated.

"Well..." I chewed my lip. "She'll find out when she gets home from work," I said in a small voice. "I left her a note."

Angela's mouth fell open. "You left her a note?" she screeched. "I thought you said last night you talked to her."

"I did talk to her. It's just..." I looked down at the floor. "Her shower's this weekend. So, she said I couldn't come."

"She said you couldn't come, but you came anyway? And you *lied* about it to *me?*" Her eyes widened.

Tears welled in my eyes, threatening to spill down my cheeks. I felt ashamed. I wasn't just lying to my mom. I was lying to my best friend too.

"I'm sorry! But this was my only chance to come to Minnesota. I just—"

"What's going on here?" Andrew asked on his way to our table. He had a plate of bread and salad in his hand. He glanced from one of us to the other.

Please don't tell, I willed Angela. It was bad enough she was mad at me. I didn't want Andrew to know I'd snuck away like some bratty little kid. And I certainly didn't want him to take me back home.

Angela looked at me like she didn't even know me. Finally, she shook her head and said, "Nothing." She spun on her heel and went to get some pizza.

The three of us ate in silence. I could feel Andrew glancing from one of us to the other, wondering what was up. But I kept my head pointed at my plate. I hated having anyone mad at me, but it felt especially bad when it was Angela.

When we finished eating, Andrew drove over to a gas station across the street. Angela played more Zombie Marbles on her phone and avoided all eye contact with me, so I took out my book. Then we were on our way again. It was a silent ride, except for Andrew's music in the front seat.

I tried to concentrate on my book, but that was hard to do when Angela's anger was taking up the whole back seat.

I stared out the window and watched the cornfields go by. I should've told her the truth last night. I should've told her my mom said no.

But would I have any chance of seeing my dad in the next few days if I had? Probably not.

"Welcome to Minnesota," Andrew said as we passed a big sign that said Minnesota Welcomes You.

I glanced at Angela, but she still wouldn't look up from her phone. Were things going to be weird between us now the whole time we were here?

I turned back to my window. The countryside was just as dull in southern Minnesota as it was in Iowa. The land was maybe a little flatter. On either side of the road, miles and miles of farmland stretched as far as the eye could see.

Finally, Angela poked my arm. "Hey," she said.

I turned. She didn't look quite as mad as she did earlier, but she didn't look like she'd forgiven me, either.

"I understand why you lied," Angela said carefully. "You were desperate. People who are desperate do desperate things."

I couldn't argue with that.

"You never would have lied to me about anything else. At least, I don't think you would have."

I shook my head. I definitely wouldn't have lied to her about anything else.

"But ever since you started this with your dad, you're like a whole different person."

"No, I'm not."

"Yes, you are. You're so obsessed. And, well, don't take this the wrong way, Sam..." She shifted in her seat. She seemed to be searching for just the right way to say it. "As your best friend, I have to tell you you're sort of gullible. I mean, you believe everything. You fall for stuff that ordinary people don't fall for."

"I do not!"

"You do too!"

I crossed my arms. "Maybe it looks that way to you because you're a half-empty kind of person and I'm a half-full kind of person."

Angela looked at me like I was speaking a foreign language. "What?"

But it made perfect sense to me. "It's how we look at the world," I went on. "You see a glass as half empty. I see the same glass as half full. I'm an optimist. You're a pessimist." It was the main difference between us.

Angela thought about that for a moment. "Maybe," she admitted. "But so what? At least I'm grounded in reality."

"Grounded in reality?" I cried. Then, remembering we weren't alone, I lowered my voice. "You're so grounded in reality, you won't even give your dad a chance. It's like here we are on the way, and you're sitting there like you're expecting your dad to pop up out of nowhere and tell you he changed his mind: that you guys can't come after all."

Angela shrugged. "It wouldn't surprise me."

"Nothing surprises you. Nothing bad, anyway."

"That's right. And I can deal with that. But what about you, Sam? What's going to happen when you come face to face with your father and you discover he's not the knight in shining armor you think he is?"

"I don't know," I said honestly. What else could I say?

I had to find out the truth about my dad and my sister. It was more important to me than anything else. More important than missing my mom's shower, more important than lying to Angela, and more important than what was going to happen to me if it turned out I was wrong about all of this.

Chapter 13

Andrew turned the music off as we started down the hill into Hill Valley. "You guys awake?" he asked. "We're almost there."

"We're awake," Angela said. She sat up a little straighter and stared out the window.

"So, this is where you used to live," I said. We passed a school, then a row of fast-food places and a park. "Looks like a nice town."

No response.

I tapped Angela on the shoulder. "You okay?"

"Yeah," she said, her forehead pressed against the window. "It's just weird to be back. Everything looks so different."

"Tell me about it," Andrew said as he glanced over at the phone he had clamped to the dashboard. Google Maps was up on the screen.

"In a quarter mile, make a left turn on 7th Street," Andrew's phone directed.

"Have you guys been to your father's house before?" I asked.

Angela snorted. "We used to live there."

"Oh." She'd never told me her dad lived in her old house.

"Dad bought Mom out when we moved to Iowa," Andrew explained.

We turned onto a nice tree-lined street. The houses were bigger than my house, but not huge. And not fancy. They were just regular nice houses. Bikes and scooters rested in front of several of them.

"You have arrived at your destination," Andrew's phone said as he stopped in front of a tall white house with red trim. A large porch stretched across the whole front of the house.

It had been three hours since we'd stopped at Pizza Hut, so I was pretty anxious to get out of the car and stretch, not to mention go to the bathroom. But Angela and Andrew took their sweet time getting out of the car. They both stared at the house as though they'd never seen it before.

"What's the matter?" I asked, glancing over at the house. I didn't see anything out of the ordinary.

"Our house is supposed to be blue," Angela said, slamming her car door.

"It's been a while since we've been here," Andrew said. "I'm sure this isn't the only thing that's different."

The door to the house swung open and a little boy with curly blond hair toddled out onto the porch and grinned. A woman with matching curly hair followed close behind. She reminded me of a toy poodle, kind of small and nervous.

"Well, hello there." She scooped up the little boy in her arms and clomped down the stairs to greet us. "You made it." Her smile felt a little too big for her mouth.

"Hi, Noreen," Andrew said. He had a pretty fake smile on his face too.

Angela didn't say anything.

Noreen carefully set the little boy down on the grass and he toddled over to me. "Baaah?" he said. He had the bluest eyes I'd ever seen.

"Cameron wants you to play ball with him, Angela," Noreen said to me.

What? Did she think *I* was Angela?

"She's not Angela," Angela spoke right up. "I am. That's my friend, Sam."

Angela sort of sidestepped around Cameron, trying not to look at him. But I could tell she was checking him out through the corner of her eye.

"Oh, yes, of course," Noreen said, her cheeks flushed with embarrassment. She came over and shook my hand. "It's nice to meet you, Sam." I noticed I was the only one of the three of us that Noreen touched.

"Goodness, I should've known which of you was Angela," Noreen said. "It hasn't been *that* long since we've seen you."

But obviously it had been. Angela and I don't look anything alike. No one would ever mistake one of us for the other.

Angela grabbed my suitcase out of the trunk and handed it to me. "Where's my father?" she asked.

Noreen blinked. "At the hospital." She seemed surprised that Angela would even ask. "He doesn't get home until seven."

"But I thought...never mind," Angela said, shaking her head. She hoisted her suitcase up out of the trunk, then trudged up the front walk.

I knew exactly what she thought. She thought her father would've been here waiting for her.

"I'll text Mom to let her know we got here safe and sound," Andrew said as soon as we stepped inside. I felt a little funny when he did that, like I should be calling my mom to let her know I'd arrived safely too. But unless I wanted to get yelled at, there was no point in doing that.

"Don't mind the mess," Noreen said, stepping over a little kid's basketball toy. Their living room reminded me of Bob's mother's living room, except there was a lot more kid stuff. Toys overflowed the shelves around the fireplace and littered the whole floor.

Noreen showed us all where we would be sleeping. Andrew got the couch in the basement. And Angela and I got a room with blue-and-white flowered wallpaper. There were two twin beds with matching white bedspreads, a night table, and a dresser. Other than that, the room was bare.

"Why don't you two get settled," Noreen said with another uneasy smile. "I'm going to go work on dinner." She seemed eager to leave us.

"We don't even get my old room," Angela grumbled once Noreen was gone. "We get the *guest* room. I suppose the kid has my old room."

She marched across the hall and yanked open the door. But that room was obviously a computer room, not a little kid's room.

Angela checked the next room. "Okay. I guess he's got Andrew's old room. That makes sense," she said, her eyes taking in the sailboat wallpaper. "This is a boy's room. But my room…"

She wandered back to the computer room, yet didn't venture inside. It was like there was an electric wire stretched across the threshold. "This room used to be pink." Now it had wood paneling.

Poor Angela. I could only imagine how she felt.

* * *

I jumped when a phone rang somewhere in the house.

Angela and I were still in the guest room. We were using Angela's phone to text with our friends back home while we waited for her dad to get home from the hospital.

"I bet that's my father calling to say he's going to be late," Angela said.

I didn't think it was Angela's dad on the phone. I had a feeling it was my mom. It was almost five o'clock. She would've gotten my note by now.

But apparently it wasn't either my mom or Angela's dad because nobody ever came to tell either of us we had a phone call. And within about ten minutes, Angela's dad came home.

Angela flew down the stairs.

A guy who I assumed was her father stood at the foot of the stairs with a grocery bag that smelled like roast chicken. He was taller than I'd pictured him. And very important looking with neatly combed dark hair, a plain white shirt, and a tie.

"Well, look who's here," he said with a stiff smile. He handed the bag to Noreen, then placed each arm awkwardly around Angela and Andrew without really hugging them. Couldn't he see that Angela wanted a real hug? At least he didn't hug Cameron, either. He just sort of ruffled the little boy's hair and said, "Hey, big guy!"

"Dadadadadada!" squealed Cameron.

I guess Mr. Hunter wasn't real big on hugging.

"This is my friend, Sam." Angela introduced us.

"It's nice to meet you, Sam." He shook my hand and practically broke every bone in it, he had such a strong grip.

"Hi," I said as though my hand wasn't killing me at all. "Thanks for letting me come with Angela."

"We're glad you could come," he said formally.

"Let's go sit down before the dinner gets cold." Noreen ushered everyone toward the kitchen and I massaged my sore hand.

I sat next to Angela. Andrew and Cameron sat across from us. Their dad and Noreen sat at opposite ends of the table. Noreen leaned over and turned on some classical music.

Angela and her brother exchanged a look, but I didn't know what it meant.

"Well." Mr. Hunter glanced around the table at Andrew, Angela, and me. "What do you kids think you'll want to do while you're here?"

I knew exactly what I wanted to do!

"There are a lot of things to choose from," Noreen said brightly. "There's swimming, roller-skating, movies…"

"Are you planning to take some time off work while we're here?" Angela asked casually as she passed her father the bowl of mashed potatoes.

Mr. Hunter let out a nervous laugh. "Well, I wish I could. But I have patients. You know I can't just leave them."

"Of course not." Angela kicked me under the table, then raised her right eyebrow pointedly.

I didn't know what to say or do in response.

"I figured you'd both want to see all your old friends while you're here," Mr. Hunter said. He turned to Andrew. "I ran into what's-his-name at the grocery store the other day." He glanced over at Noreen. "What *is* his name?"

Noreen was tearing a roll apart for Cameron. "You mean the Slater boy? Brian?"

"That's right. Brian. He's working at Cub Foods now. I told him you were coming up this week, Andrew. He said he'd love to see you."

"Cool," Andrew replied, shoving a forkful of potatoes into his mouth. "I can show him my car."

"And I'd be happy to drop you girls off anywhere you'd like to go," Noreen said. "As long as you're willing to plan around Cameron's nap."

Ha! I wondered whether she'd be willing to "drop us off" in front of 7430 Sheridan Avenue South in Richland?

Later, when Angela and I were getting ready for bed in the guest room, Angela said, "I don't know why my dad even agreed to let us come up here if he isn't going to spend any time with us."

"Maybe it's like he said. He thought you'd want to see your old friends," I suggested.

Angela pulled her bed spread down. "I was in second grade when we moved away from here," she said. "I don't really have friends here anymore. Besides, I came to see him. Not my old friends."

The phone rang and I stopped breathing. Someone picked it up on the first ring. I didn't move for a full thirty seconds.

Then I relaxed. By then I figured if it was my mom, somebody would've called me.

"Well, then maybe we can see if we find the bus station tomorrow," I said, crawling into bed. "I want to see if there's a bus to Richland and find out what time it leaves and what time it gets back."

Angela plopped down on her bed. "You're really going to go up there? By yourself?"

Was Angela really so surprised? "That's why I came here," I said. "Well, that and to hang out with you. Do you want to come with me?"

Angela shrugged. "Maybe. It's not like there's anything better to do around here. I know where the bus station is. Andrew and I took the bus up here last time we visited my dad. It's just a few blocks away. How much do you think a bus ticket would cost?"

Before I could answer, there was a knock at our door. "Yeah?" Angela called.

Noreen opened the door and poked her head in. "Telephone for you, Sam," she said, handing me a phone. She pinched her lips together in disapproval.

I gulped. Uh oh.

Noreen left, closing the door softly behind her. Angela gave me an I'm-glad-I'm-not-you look, then reached for her earbuds.

I slowly raised the phone to my ear, gripping it with both hands. "H-hello?" I said shakily.

"You are in big trouble, young lady!"

"Mom, I can explain—"

"Can you? Can you really? Well, start talking, Sam, because I'd love to hear how you ended up in Hill Valley, Minnesota, when I specifically told you you couldn't go."

What? She wanted me to tell her right now?

I gulped again. "Well," I began in a small voice. "I-I can't tell you right now. But I promise I'll tell you when I get back to Clearwater—"

"That's going to be sooner than you think," Mom spat at me. "I already spoke with Angela's stepmother. They'll take you to the bus station tomorrow morning and you're going to be on the eight-twenty bus to Cedar Rapids. I'll have to leave work a few minutes early, but I'll be in Cedar Rapids when you arrive at three forty-five."

"Mom, no!" I couldn't go home! Not yet! Not until I'd been to Richland.

"Don't 'Mom, no' me. If it wasn't so late, I'd drive up there and get you myself right now. Unfortunately, it took a while to get a hold of Anne to find out where you were. Your phone seems to be conveniently turned off. Funny, Anne was under the impression you had permission to go to Minnesota. She was pretty surprised to find out otherwise."

I couldn't worry about what Angela's mom thought of me right now. "Mom, you have to let me stay—" I begged. I never in a million years thought she'd make me go home.

"You're not staying, Sam! You're going to get on that bus in the morning and come home. And it'll be a long time before you even think about going anywhere else."

Chapter 14

The first thing I noticed about the Hill Valley bus station was the smell. The whole place smelled like fried eggs. But even though I hadn't eaten anything that morning, I didn't feel at all hungry.

I shuffled along in line until it was my turn at the ticket counter. "One-way ticket to Cedar Rapids, Iowa," I mumbled to the guy behind the counter. I handed him my mom's debit card.

Angela and her dad waited for me over by the map of Minnesota. They both stared at that map as though it was the most interesting thing in the world.

The ticket guy handed me my mom's card and my ticket. "Your bus is already here. Lane 1. But we won't be boarding for another half an hour. Next?"

I picked up my ticket and my suitcase, then moped over to Angela and her dad. *It was over.* I was heading home with no more information than I'd come with. Plus, I was going to see some major trouble when I got there. Probably more trouble than I'd ever seen before in my entire life.

Angela's dad smiled uncomfortably. He checked his watch. "You don't need me to wait around until the bus leaves, do you?" he asked me. "I really should be getting in to the hospital."

"Oh, no," I said right away. Something about Angela's dad made me want to stand at attention. "I have my ticket." I held it up. "The bus is here. I'll be fine."

Angela's dad looked relieved. "Okay, then," he said, holding out his hand. "It was nice meeting you, Sam. I hope you have a nice ride back home."

"Thanks," I said as he about killed my hand again.

He started to walk away when Angela called out, "Wait! Don't I get to say good-bye to Sam before we leave?"

He turned and glanced quizzically at his daughter. "We?"

"Well, yeah," Angela's voice dropped. "Aren't you going to drop me off back at...your house before you go to the hospital?"

Her dad laughed. "Angela, the house is only a few blocks from here. You can stay and see your friend off, then you can walk home." He turned back around and headed out to the parking lot like the busy, important man that he probably was.

I guess I didn't think it was *that* big of a deal. Angela and I were planning on walking to the bus station by ourselves anyway before my mom called. So, it couldn't have been that far. But Angela was ticked. "It would serve him right if I got mugged walking back by myself," she grumbled.

"In this town?" I cried. Hill Valley wasn't any bigger than Clearwater.

"It happens," Angela said.

There was no place to sit down in the bus station except at the breakfast counter. And it didn't seem right to sit there if we weren't going to eat anything. So, we wandered outside.

It smelled even worse out here. Diesel fuel.

Another bus was just pulling in. It said Mall of America in the little screen above the driver. I knew the Mall of America was near Minneapolis. I wondered how far it was from Richland.

Angela leaned back against the brick building and sighed. "I ought to just hop on that bus and go to the Mall of America today," she said.

I sighed. "Me too. I'm already in trouble. What's a little more?"

Angela looked at me. "I could do it if I wanted to. My dad gave me eighty bucks this morning. He told me to go to the mall and buy myself something nice. On him." She snorted.

Whoa! Eighty bucks? "So, do it," I said with a shrug.

"Go to the Mall of America?" Angela asked. "Without permission?"

"No," I laughed. "Go to the mall here and buy yourself something nice."

"Oh. Right." Angela nodded knowingly. Then she raised her eyebrow at me. "You don't think I'd do it, do you?"

"Do what?"

"Get on that bus and go to the Mall of America."

Uh, no. There was no way Angela would do that. She was the responsible one. I was the crazy one.

Angela shrugged. "Why don't you go in there," she tilted her head toward the bus station, "and see if you can find out whether you can get where you want to go in Richland from the Mall of America."

My eyes about popped out of my head when she said that.

"What?" Angela said with a shrug. "I thought that was why you came here. You wanted to go see if this guy in Richland is your dad and find out whether he has your sister." I saw a mischievous look in Angela's eyes that I'd never seen there before.

"Well, I do, but..." But what? There was no one here to make sure I got on the right bus. And like I'd just told Angela, I was already in a heap of trouble. What was a little more? It would be totally worth it if I found my dad and my sister.

We hurried back inside to talk to the guy at the ticket counter. It turned out the Mall of America bus just went to the Mall of America. But we checked Google and found out we could catch a city bus at the Mall of America that would take us over to Penn Avenue. We'd stay on the city bus until we got to 74th Street. Then we'd walk three blocks to Sheridan Avenue and we'd be there. Piece of cake.

Angela and I looked at each other and grinned.

"What do you think?" Angela asked.

"Let's do it!" I said.

I half-expected the ticket guy to refuse to let me change my ticket without a parent's permission. But there hadn't been a parent standing there when I'd bought the ticket in the first place. So, no problem. I changed my one-way ticket to Cedar Rapids to a round-trip ticket to the Mall of America. And Angela bought another round-trip ticket to the Mall of America. We'd arrive at eleven-thirty and get back at nine o'clock tonight.

"My dad's going to kill me when we get back," Angela said with a huge smile on her face.

"Well, maybe we can have a joint funeral because I'm already dead," I said as the bus to Cedar Rapids pulled away without me. I looked at Angela. "I suppose I should let my mom know she doesn't have to pick me up."

"You're going to call her?" Angela said.

I shook my head. "I'm going to call her work." I knew she'd probably be with patients and wouldn't be able to talk. It's an advantage to having a mom who was a nurse.

When the receptionist came on the line, I said, "Hi, this is Samantha Wright. I'm Suzanne Sperling's daughter. Could you please tell her not to pick me up in Cedar Rapids? Tell her I'm not on the bus."

"Anything else, Samantha?" the woman asked in a bored voice.

"No, that'll do it," I said. Then I hit the power button on my phone.

"The bus to Mall of America is now boarding in lane 3," a voice came over the intercom.

Angela and I looked at each other and giggled. I didn't know about Angela, but I felt like a wild animal escaping from the zoo. Giddy with excitement, I grabbed my suitcase and Angela and I ran outside and climbed onto the bus.

* * *

The bus stopped in every piddly town between Hill Valley and the Mall of America. In fact, some of the places we stopped were so small I could hardly believe they really were towns. All the starting and stopping—plus the bus fumes and the perfume of the lady in front of us—made my stomach feel queasy.

Angela nudged me. "You don't look so good, Sam. Are you okay?"

"I think I'm bus sick," I moaned, clutching my stomach.

"Open the window."

"Are you kidding?" I cried. "That would totally mess up my hair."

Angela shrugged. "Personally, I'd rather have messy hair than smell like puke."

She had a point. I cracked the window and a cool blast of fresh air hit me right in the nose. Every time a wave of nausea came over me, I stuck my nose in the crack of open window and inhaled deep breaths of fresh air until I felt better. When we reached the outskirts of the Twin Cities there was enough traffic around us that the air outside the bus probably wasn't much fresher than the air inside the bus. But I did manage to make it all the way to the Mall of America without throwing up.

Wow! Angela and I knew the mall would be big, but we had no idea it was *this* big. All we could do was stare at it in awe. You have to understand, for two girls from Iowa, the Mall of America was mind-boggling. More than five hundred stores under one roof?

The bus let us out on the lowest level of a big parking ramp. The guy I talked to at the Hill Valley bus station said we'd be able to see where the city buses picked up when we got off the Hill Valley bus. And sure enough, there they were across the parking lot. But now that I was here, I wasn't sure I was ready to go over there and get on the next bus. I wasn't sure I was ready to face whatever I might find at 7430 Sheridan Avenue South.

Angela was already halfway across the parking ramp. She turned when she realized I wasn't with her. "What's the matter?" she asked. "Don't you want to do this?"

I blinked. "Of course I do," I said, hurrying to catch up with her. This was why I was here.

We went down the line checking for the #4 bus. That was the one that was supposed to take us to Penn Avenue. "This is it," Angela said, stopping in front of a big white bus.

The door opened and we climbed on. "Are you going to Penn Avenue?" Angela asked the bus driver just to be sure.

He was an old guy with dark skin, glasses, and clumps of white hair that looked like pieces of cotton stuck to the sides of his head. He didn't answer out loud, just nodded once.

We put our money in the slot, then found a seat in the middle of the bus. We weren't even moving yet, but already I felt bus sick again. I wiped my sweaty palms on my shorts and leaned my head back against my seat.

"So, what's the plan?" Angela crossed one leg over the other. "We'll just go up to that house, ring the bell, and see what happens?"

"Pretty much."

"What if nobody answers the door?"

"I don't know."

As the bus started out across the Mall of America parking lot, my stomach heaved.

"Okay, what if someone does answer the door?" Angela persisted. "What then?"

"I don't know!" I wasn't in the mood to talk. I just wanted to rest my head against the hard seat and think. Because believe me, those questions and more were swirling around in my head.

It was weird. All along, I was the one pushing forward, trying to find my dad. And Angela was pulling me back. Now Angela was the one pushing forward. To tell you the truth, I was starting to have some major doubts about this whole thing. I mean, running off to Minnesota without my mom's permission? Getting on the Mall of America bus instead of the Cedar Rapids bus? Taking another bus across town to a total stranger's house?

What was I thinking?

I turned to the window. There was so much traffic here. So many cars, so many horns. So many buildings. So many people. And here we were, two girls alone in a big city. We could get hit by a car or something up here and no one would ever know because no one even knew we were here. Unlike Clearwater or Hill Valley, there were real dangers in a place like Minneapolis.

Then I remembered the voice mail recording and my hairs stood on end once more. That was my dad's voice on the recording. I was sure of it. And I still had this feeling my sister could somehow still be alive.

I had come a long way to find out the truth. So, when I saw the sign for 74th Street, I reached up and pulled the cord above the window. A bell rang and the bus slowed.

Was I ready for this?

By the time the bus finally stopped, we were up to 72nd Street.

"We're going to have to walk back a couple blocks, then cut over to Sheridan Avenue," Angela said, staring at directions on her phone.

"I know." I didn't care. I needed the few extra minutes to calm myself down.

Angela peered at me. "Are you okay?" she asked as cars whizzed past on the street.

I shrugged. "I'm scared," I said in a small voice.

Angela took my hand. "I don't blame you," she said. "But remember, you're a half-full kind of person. Whatever happens, you should be able to handle it."

This was all just a big adventure to Angela. She was

away from home. Away from her dad. She didn't know whether I was right about my dad living at 7430 Sheridan Avenue South and my sister possibly living there too. For her, it didn't matter whether I was right or not. She was just along for the ride.

Me, I was pretty sure I was right. But what if I was wrong? Or what if I *was* right? At the moment, I wasn't sure which possibility scared me more.

We crossed the street, then started up 74th Street. The houses around here were small and sad looking. There were no flowers out front. Just lots of scraggly bushes, an occasional big, ugly pine tree, and patches of dead grass. A couple of the houses had cracked windows. Many of them needed paint. Did my dad really live around here? Or had he lived here until a few days ago?

There was a cemetery up ahead. I hated cemeteries. Why would anyone want to live so close to a cemetery?

"I don't think this street goes all the way through," Angela said. "Should we turn here and see if we can get to Sheridan Avenue going this way?"

"Okay," I said. We made one turn, then another. Finally, we came to Sheridan Avenue. Sweat dribbled down my back. My stomach felt funny again.

At least the houses looked a little better along here. They were still small, but they looked more like our little house back in Clearwater. The grass even seemed greener down here and a few houses had flowers out front.

"It shouldn't be much farther," Angela said. "What's the number again?"

"7430."

There were only two houses on this side of the street, then a playground and what looked like an elementary school. But across the street there was 7418...7424. And then 7430.

I stopped. It was just an ordinary brown house with a big picture window and two tiny bedroom windows. One of the garage windows was boarded up.

Angela grabbed my arm. "Well, let's go ring the bell and see what happens."

I don't know how I even made it across the street. You know how when you stare at something too hard, the whole image sort of melts apart? That's what was happening to me. Plus, my arms and legs were so tingly that I didn't think I could walk. But somehow, I found myself standing at the front door.

"Go ahead. Ring the bell," Angela said.

My heart raced. My stomach lurched. I was in serious danger of throwing up. But I stuck out a shaky finger and pressed the button. I heard the bell ring inside the house and a dog came running to the door. That was unexpected!

"Someone lives here," Angela said.

"Someone with a dog," I added.

The dog scratched at the door and barked at us. But no one yelled at him to stop and no one came to the door.

A fuzzy memory popped into my head. My mom and dad arguing.

"Come on, Suzanne. It's just a dog."

"I don't want a dog. Dogs are too much responsibility."

Angela lifted the top on the black mailbox beside the front door.

"What are you doing?" I asked.

"Checking to see whether Joseph Wright really does live here and whether he's picked up his mail recently."

There was some mail in the box, but not a lot. Ads from JCPenney and Home Depot. A couple of bills. All addressed to Joseph Wright. There was definitely a Joseph Wright living here. Was there a Sarah Wright here too?

"What should we do?" Angela asked.

Now that I knew for sure he was here, I had to see him. "Wait, I guess," I said.

"He's probably at work," Angela said.

"Probably," I agreed. "Hopefully he works an early shift somewhere and gets off mid-afternoon."

We walked over to the playground across the street and plopped down on the merry-go-round where we had a good view of the house. And I could set my suitcase down for a while. If anyone came in or out, we would see them.

I had to admit it got a little boring just sitting there. Not to mention hot. But what did I expect? It was the beginning of August. Still, I was determined to wait it out. My dad or Joseph—I wasn't sure what to call him— would come back eventually. And I wanted to be there when he did.

I ran my fingers through my hair. Oh no! After two bus rides and an hour or so sitting in the hot sun, my hair was probably a disaster! I *so* wanted to look good the first time I met my dad. I whipped out my comb and gently pulled it through my hair.

"Your hair's fine," Angela said, rolling her eyes.

"Really?"

"Well, considering we're sitting out here in 85-degree heat, it's probably as good as it's going to get."

"Gee, thanks," I said. I kept right on combing.

It was almost two o'clock. My stomach growled.

"Should we go get something to eat and then come back?" Angela asked.

"I don't want to leave," I said, finally putting my comb away. I knew that if I took my eyes off the house for one second, I'd miss something.

"We'll only be gone for a little bit," Angela said. "We'll come right back. We can even ring the doorbell again, in case we missed him."

I shook my head. "You go if you want. I'm staying here."

"I don't think we should split up," Angela said. So, we stayed where we were.

After a while, Angela got up and started walking around. "I have to go to the bathroom," she said. "Do you?"

I did. Kind of. But I still didn't want to leave. "I'm okay."

I noticed there was a door open at the school. "You could probably use the bathroom in there," I told Angela, nodding toward the school.

She glanced at the open door, then back at me. "Okay. You sure you don't want to come with me?"

"Nah." I shook my head again.

But once she was gone, I wished I had gone with her. It was kind of creepy sitting there by myself. I could hear birds chirping and wind rustling through the trees. There was absolutely nobody around.

I felt better when Angela came back. She held out two bags from Taco Bell. One had food in it, the other drinks.

"Where'd you get that?" I asked.

"Over there." She pointed to a busier street on the other side of the school. "Across the street."

We were so hungry we gobbled up the tacos and nachos in about two minutes flat. And of course after I drank the pop I *really* had to go to the bathroom. I knew I could run into that school like Angela did, but I didn't want to. I was sure that the minute I left, my dad would come home. So, I crossed my legs and tried not to think about it.

Angela checked her watch. "We're going to have to head back to the Mall of America in an hour or so. We don't want to miss the bus back to Hill Valley."

I didn't say anything. She was right, of course. But how could I leave if my dad hadn't come back yet?

"Sam? Did you hear what I said?"

"Yes!"

"I mean, this has been fun and everything, but we don't want to be stuck here all night. If this guy hasn't come back by five-thirty, we have to leave." Responsible

Angela was back.

"I know!" I said. To tell you the truth, though, I wasn't sure I would be willing to leave at five-thirty. Not if my dad hadn't come back.

Before I could argue the point any further, I noticed this person around my age coming toward us. I say person because their whitish blond hair was cropped so short I honestly couldn't tell whether it was a boy or a girl. But as the person drew closer, I could tell she was a girl because she had...well, she had breasts.

She wore a softball uniform and carried an equipment bag. There was a smudge of dirt on her cheek. Goose-bumps dotted my arms and the back of my neck.

I can't explain it, but I just knew.

"Sarah?"

I didn't even realize I'd spoken out loud until the girl turned and looked at me.

Then I knew for sure. "Oh my God!" I gasped. "You really are alive."

Chapter 15

The girl looked at me like I had three heads. "Huh?"

I moved toward her. "You're Sarah, right?" I said.

"No." The girl shook her head. "My name's T. J." She glowered at me, chomping on a big wad of strawberry bubblegum.

T. J.? No! She was Sarah. She had to be. We were about the same age. Same height. We had the exact same shade of whitish blond hair. She wore her hair totally different than I wore mine. She wore it totally different than I ever *would* wear mine. But...she was Sarah. She had to be.

Angela grabbed my arm. "I don't think this girl is your sister, Sam," she said. "She looks too—" Angela looked the girl up and down. "*Not like you* to be your sister."

The girl snorted. "I don't have a sister," she said as she started to walk away.

"But—" I wiggled out of Angela's grasp and started after the other girl. She looked annoyed to find me walking beside her, staring at her face. She had kind of a tomboyish look about her. There wasn't a single speck of makeup on her face at all. But aside from that, I was sure I saw a resemblance between us.

Okay, maybe we didn't look exactly alike, but we were definitely related. That much was obvious. Maybe we were fraternal twins instead of identical twins. Didn't she see it too?

"You turned when I said Sarah," I said to the girl. Didn't that mean something?

She looked at me like yeah, so?

"You did!" I insisted.

"She turned because you were talking to her," Angela said as though I were a five-year-old. "You'd turn too if you were walking across the park and someone started talking to you." She smiled nervously at T. J. "Sorry we bothered you," she said as she tried to lead me away.

The girl shrugged like I was just another nutcase, then continued across the park.

She wasn't Sarah?

I looked at Angela. "I was so sure."

"I know."

"No, really," I said. "The moment I saw that girl…" She was almost to the street now. "I just—I don't know. I felt a connection."

"You wanted her to be your sister," Angela said. "You wanted it to be true, so you thought you felt something when you really didn't."

But I *did* feel something. Even now, watching her cross the street, I still felt it. That girl was my sister. Didn't she feel it too? A connection to me? Why didn't she look back?

"Come on." Angela touched my arm. "We should head back to the Mall of America."

My eyes were glued to the girl's back. Where was she going?

She was going to my dad's house!

"Hey!" I yelled, running after her. "Wait a minute!"

"Sam!" Angela cried.

The girl turned as I barreled across the street. She had the screen door open and was about to insert a key in the lock when I came running up behind her.

"You live here?" I gasped, struggling to catch my breath.

She looked at me like what-are-you-babbling-about-now, like I was some pesky mosquito that wouldn't go away.

"Is your last name Wright?" I tried again. "Is Joseph Wright your dad?"

She let the screen door close, then planted a hand on her hip. "Who are you?" she asked.

Her eyes were exactly the same shade of green as mine. She also had a pointy nose. Just like mine. And her right ear was pierced two times while her left ear was pierced just once. Talk about weird. That was exactly how my ears were pierced.

She had a mole on the left side of her chin. I had one on the right side of mine.

"Come on, Sam! You can't just—" Angela screeched to a halt beside me. She had my suitcase in her hand and her eyes darted back and forth between me and the other girl, whoever she was. Then she frowned. "You know, you guys do look kind of alike."

Kind of? If I chopped off most of my hair to look like hers, we would look like *twins*. I could tell by the confusion in the other girl's eyes that she finally saw it now too.

"Who are you?" she asked again.

"I'm Sam," I said as though that explained it all.

She looked at me blankly. "Sam who?"

"Samantha Wright."

Still no reaction.

"Doesn't that name mean anything to you?" I asked.

She shrugged. "Not really."

I didn't get it. How could she totally forget me?

"Is your last name Wright?" I asked.

"Yes."

"And is your dad's name Joseph Wright?"

"Yes."

"Joseph Wright is my dad!" I said.

She didn't look convinced.

"I heard his voice on your voice mail."

The girl smirked. "You mean our answering machine?"

"Whatever!" I didn't care how they got messages off their phone. "It's him! I know it is!" Speaking of phones... "Why is your phone disconnected?"

She frowned. "It's not."

"Yes, it is. I called and left a message on your voice ma—I mean, answering machine. But when I called back, the phone had been disconnected."

"Our phone number got changed—"

Aha! "How come?"

"I don't know. Ask the phone company." She looked at me like quit-bugging-me, but I couldn't stop now.

"You're my sister. My *twin* sister. Can't you tell? We have the same eyes and the same nose and we even pierced our ears the same way!"

"Easy, Sam," Angela said, swinging my suitcase in front of her. "You're freaking her out."

I was. The girl, Sarah or T. J. or whoever she was, looked nervous. Which was funny because I could tell she was the kind of girl who didn't take crap from anyone. The kind of girl who punched first and asked questions later. The kind of girl who was very different from me.

Angela switched my suitcase to her left hand and held out her right hand. "Hi," she said with a smile. "I'm Angela, Sam's friend."

The girl shook Angela's hand weakly, but didn't smile.

"We could probably clear this whole thing up really quick if you had a photo of your dad or something," Angela went on. "Something so Sam can see for sure whether she's got the right Joseph Wright."

"I know I've got the right one," I insisted. I could not take my eyes off this girl. "And I also know...you're my sister."

"Well, let her show you a picture anyway," Angela said. "Just to be sure. Do you have one on your phone?" she asked T. J.

T. J. sighed. "Believe it or not, not everyone in the

world has a cell phone," she said. She turned to me. "But if Joe really is your dad, then there's no way I could be your sister."

"How do you know?"

"Because he's not my real dad."

"He's not?" Angela and I said at the same time.

"No." She shook her head. "Not that it's any of your business. Sometimes people think he's my dad because we have the same blond hair. But Joe was my real dad's best friend. He adopted me when my parents died."

"Your parents died?" I repeated. This wasn't making any sense.

"They died when I was little. I don't really remember them."

"Did you ever have a sister?" I asked desperately.

T. J. blew a bubble with her gum, then sucked it back in. "No. I had a brother. An older brother. But he died when my parents did."

"I'm sorry," Angela said.

T. J. shrugged. "Like I said, I don't really remember them. It was a long time ago. What makes you think Joe is your dad?"

I launched into the whole story, beginning with the psychic and the newspaper clippings and ending with the disconnected phone. I had to admit, the whole thing sounded pretty lame when I said it out loud.

"So...when you saw me, you thought I was your sister?" T. J. asked. She clearly wasn't buying it.

"Well—"

"Look, I can probably find a picture somewhere in the house," T. J. said abruptly. "You can at least see if Joe is your dad. But if he's not, I want you to leave, okay? It's been kind of a crappy day."

"Okay," I agreed. That was all I really wanted anyway. To find out if this Joseph Wright is my dad or not.

Angela and I stayed on the driveway while T. J. turned back to her house. As soon as she pulled the screen door open, the dog started barking. "Hang on, Sherlock! I'm coming."

Both Angela and I whipped our heads around. "Sherlock?" I ran toward her. "Your dog's name is Sherlock?"

T. J. grinned. "Yeah." She opened the door and this shaggy mass of white fur leaped at her legs. T. J. bent down and picked him up. His whole hind end wiggled in her arms and he licked her neck.

"Isn't he the greatest?" T. J. asked, bringing the dog over to me so I could pet him. "He's a West Highland terrier."

I gave the dog an obligatory pat on the head.

"We got him when he was just a pup and he was so nosy! Into everything. That's why we named him Sherlock."

"My cat's name is Sherlock," I said.

T. J.'s smile froze to her face. "What?"

"It's true," Angela nodded.

"I got him when I was ten. I named him after Sherlock Holmes."

"That's...weird," T. J. said, hugging her dog close to

her chest. I could tell she didn't like it that our pets had the same name.

"Really weird," Angela agreed.

T. J. bit her bottom lip like she was debating whether or not to say something. She took a step closer to me. "You want to hear something that's even weirder?" she asked.

I swallowed hard. "What?"

T. J. hesitated for just a second. "Your name is Sam, right?"

"Well, my real name is Samantha. But everyone calls me Sam."

T. J.'s eyes locked on mine and she said, "My brother? The one who died? His name was Sam too."

Chapter 16

I shivered. T. J. didn't have a sister, but she had a brother named Sam. And he died a long time ago just like my sister did. How weird was that?

"When's your birthday?" I asked, shifting my weight from one foot to the other. We were still standing in T. J.'s driveway.

T. J. eyed me warily. "August 26," she replied.

Okay, that proved it. We had to be twins!

"That's my birthday too!" I told her excitedly. "You're going to be fourteen, right?"

T. J. shook her head. "Thirteen," she said, chomping her gum.

I blinked. "Thirteen? You mean you're only twelve now?"

She nodded.

That couldn't be right.

"What grade are you going into?" Angela asked.

"Eighth."

And I was going into ninth. "But we have the same birthday," I protested. "The same birthday, same hair

color, same eye color, same pet names, same dad—"
Even though he was her *adopted* dad, I was sure it was the
same dad. It had to be.

"But T. J.'s a year younger than you," Angela pointed
out. "And she's adopted. And we haven't actually seen a
picture of this guy yet. We don't know for sure that he's
your dad."

T. J. looked as uneasy as I felt. "Why don't you guys
come in and I'll see if I can find a picture of Joe."

"You call him Joe?" I asked.

She hesitated. "That's his name. Come on." T. J. put
the dog down and opened the front door. Sherlock scampered into the house, his tail wagging the whole way.
Angela and I followed close behind.

It was warm in the house. T. J. and Joe didn't have air
conditioning. But despite the heat, I felt chilled just being
inside their house. *My dad's house.* This was where he got up
every morning, had breakfast, went to work, came home,
had dinner, watched TV, and did whatever else he did.

The house looked totally different from our house. It
had what you'd call that "lived-in" look. None of the fur-
niture matched. There was an old caramel-colored couch
that was piled with newspapers, a couple of scratched-up
tables (one of them had a dirty glass on it), and a green
wooden rocker. There was a picture of a group of dogs
playing band instruments hanging on the wall. I couldn't
imagine any of this stuff in our house. Or in Bob's house,
for that matter.

T. J. opened a closet and pulled a photo album down

from the shelf. "Okay," she said, opening it up. "This is Joe." She pointed.

I peered over her shoulder and saw a photo of a man raking leaves. He looked older than the guy in those newspaper articles I'd found in our basement, but I recognized the hair, the eyes, the mustache. He used to tickle me with that mustache!

"That's him!" I cried, drawing in my breath. "That's my dad."

T. J. stiffened.

"Are you sure?" Angela asked.

"Positive." Too bad I didn't have that photo from the newspaper article to prove it. But I did have another photo that T. J. might want to see. I opened my purse and took out the photo of Sarah and me.

"Look at this," I said, handing it to T. J.

She stared at it so hard she practically burned a hole in it. She even stopped chewing her gum.

I could hardly breathe. "Is one of those girls you?"

T. J. didn't take her eyes off the photo. "I don't know," she said softly.

"What do you mean you don't know?" I asked. "How can you not know whether a photo is you or not?" Of course, I wasn't sure which girl in the photo was me, either.

"Let's compare it to a photo you have of yourself when you were little," Angela suggested.

"That's just it," T. J. said, raising her eyes to meet mine. "I don't have any photos of me from when I was little."

"You don't?"

She shook her head. "They all got burned in the fire."

"What fire?"

"The one that killed my parents and my brother."

I chewed my bottom lip. I didn't know what to think anymore. There were so many coincidences. But so many other things didn't quite add up.

"Where did you live with your parents and your brother?" I asked. "Did you live in Iowa?"

"Yes," T. J. said, surprised. "I was born in a town called Clearwater."

"That's where I live!" I cried.

T. J. and I just stared at one another in amazement. I'm not sure either one of us took a breath.

I cleared my throat. "When will..." I didn't know what to say. Your dad? My dad? Our dad? "When will Joe be home?" I said finally. Joe was what she called him. He was the key to this whole thing. The one who could answer all our questions.

"I don't know." She glanced at the little round clock on the wall above the kitchen table. "Before last week, he probably would've been home by now. He's a handyman, so he just works a couple hours here and a couple hours there. Whenever he's got a job, I mean. But he hasn't been home much lately because Gram's been pretty sick—"

Gram? Did she mean Grandma Wright?

"She's in a nursing home," T. J. went on. "And she's not doing very well. Joe just got a job this week too. So he's been splitting his time between the job and the nursing home. He hasn't been coming home until like nine or ten o'clock at night."

"Nine or ten at night?" Angela repeated. "We can't hang around that long. We have to get back to Hill Valley, Sam. She checked her watch, "In fact, if we don't leave soon, we're going to miss the bus!"

The last thing on my mind was catching a bus back to Hill Valley.

"I can't leave," I said. "Not until I see my dad."

"I know," Angela said. "But Sam, that's the only bus back to Hill Valley tonight. I checked. If we're not on it, how are we going to get back?"

"I could call Joe and tell him I need him to come home," T. J. offered. She still looked a little unsure about all this.

"Would you?" I asked. As far as I was concerned, the sooner he got here, the better.

"I'm only supposed to call if it's an emergency," T. J. explained. "But this is sort of an emergency."

"Go call," Angela said. "If Sam and I aren't on that last bus to Hill Valley, it will be a huge emergency!"

So, T. J. went into the kitchen to make her call. Angela and I just stood around in the living room.

"What do you think?" I whispered. "Do you think she's Sarah?"

"I don't know," Angela whispered back. "I didn't at first, but now? I don't know."

I paced back and forth. I couldn't stand still. "What makes you think it's possible?" I asked. "The fact that we look so much alike? Or that she doesn't have any pictures from when she was little? Or that she was born in Clearwater? Or that we have the same birthday?"

"I don't know. All of that together, I guess."

"He didn't answer," T. J. said as she came back into the living room. "I left a message, though. He'll come home as soon as he gets the message."

"What'd you say in the message?" I asked. Would she have just come right out and said, *"Hey, Joe. Your other daughter is here"*? And what would his reaction be? After all, if this was true—if T. J. was Sarah—then I was the daughter he'd left behind. The one he didn't want.

Why didn't he want me?

"I didn't really say anything. I just said there was a family emergency and I needed him to come home. He'll probably think it's about Gram."

My head was spinning. Grandma Wright. Dad. Sarah. T. J. It was all too much. What was going on here? What happened all those years ago?

"Should we wait in my room?" T. J. asked.

"Sure," Angela said.

"Why not," I said. We followed T. J. down the hall. Sherlock plodded along behind us, his nose to the floor.

I couldn't help but look in the other rooms we passed along the way. There was a paneled TV room, a small bathroom, my dad's bedroom…I lingered in the doorway there. *This was where my dad slept.*

The window shades were pulled and there was paneling on the walls in here too, only this paneling was darker than the stuff in the other room. It was so dark you could go to sleep right in the middle of the day. I spotted a single unmade bed against one wall and a banged-up old dresser against another. A ceiling fan hummed as it spun above. But there was nothing on the walls. Nothing that told me who this Joe Wright was or what was important to him.

"Are you coming?" T. J. poked her head out of her room and looked at me.

"Yeah." I pulled myself away from my dad's room.

When I got to T. J.'s room, I thought I was in a boy's room. There were tons of sports posters on the wall. Most of the people looked like baseball players, but there was at least one basketball player too. I didn't even know who half those people were.

"I guess you like sports, huh?" Angela said as we both sat down on the navy comforter. T. J. pulled out her desk chair and straddled it backwards, her arms resting on the top of the chair back.

"Yeah. Joe and I are into all kinds of sports."

Didn't she like any movie stars or singers? What about pictures of her friends? She didn't even have a mirror above her dresser to stick pictures of her friends in like I did. How did she do her makeup and hair without a mirror?

Speaking of hair, no doubt mine looked terrible. And I was about to meet my dad for the very first time.

I hopped up. "Do you have a flat iron I could borrow real quick?" I asked T. J. Hopefully I had time to do something with my hair before my dad got here.

"No," she said.

I frowned. "I can't borrow it?"

"I don't have one."

"You don't have a flat iron?" I gaped at her. I get why she wouldn't have a phone. Phones are expensive and I can tell she and Joe don't have a lot of money. But flat irons aren't very expensive.

She snorted. "What do I need one for?" she asked, poking at her short, spiky hair. It couldn't have been more than half an inch long anywhere on her head.

Did she always wear her hair so short?

"You look fine, Sam," Angela said in a tired voice. She pulled me back down onto T. J.'s bed.

I knew I did not look fine, but—ugh, I was sitting on something. I reached under me and—whoa!—pulled out a stuffed monkey that looked an awful lot like my monkey back home.

"Hey, where did you get this?" I asked, holding it up.

T. J. grabbed the monkey out of my hands. "My grandma made it," she said, dusting it off. Then she tossed it onto her desk, out of my reach.

"I have one just like it at home."

T. J. frowned. "You couldn't have one *just* like it. I told you, my grandma made it! It's one of a kind."

"It looks the same to me," Angela said.

I heard a voice in my head:

Do you know the Monkey Man?

Do you know the monkey man?
The monkey man? The monkey man.
Do you know the monkey man?
Who lives on Hartman Lane...

"Does Joe ever call himself the monkey man?" I asked T. J.

"The monkey man?"

"Yeah. You know that song 'Do You Know the Muffin Man'? Does Joe ever sing it as 'Do You Know the Monkey Man'?"

"Joe? Sing?" T. J. snorted. "I don't think I've ever heard him sing."

"Oh," I said, disappointed. I was sure someone had told me he was a musician.

"Do you guys play any sports?" T. J. asked.

"Sam and I both play softball," Angela said.

"Oh yeah? What positions?" T. J. asked, growing more interested.

"I play first base," Angela said.

"What about you?" T. J. looked at me.

"Oh. I'm not very good. They like to keep me out of the way, so I play right field."

Angela rolled her eyes.

"What do you mean 'out of the way'?" T. J. slapped her leg and Sherlock popped his head up. "*I* play right field. Right field is a very important position. You have to have a really good arm to play outfield."

"Sure. Whatever." No way could she convince me

Coach Frye put me in right field because of my stellar arm.

The conversation fizzled out there, and T. J. and I just sort of checked each other out without being too obvious about it. Neither one of us really knew what to say. Thank goodness for Angela. Whenever the silences stretched too long, she always came up with something for us to talk about. Like hobbies. Or school.

T. J. and I discovered we both played in band. But I played the flute, she played the tuba. I liked social studies, she liked science. We both hated English. Finally, something in common! And she didn't think it was at all strange that I could hate English class and still want to be a writer when I grew up.

"Those books they make us read?" she said, wrinkling her nose. "Bo-ring!"

"No kidding," I said. "I'm going to write way better books than those when I grow up. I'm going to write the kinds of books people actually want to read."

"Oh yeah? What kind of books?"

"Mysteries, of course. What do you want to be when you grow up?"

T. J. sat up a little straighter. "A doctor." She sounded so sure.

"Wow."

She shrugged. "I want to make a difference in the world."

"You mean you want to find a cure for cancer or something?" Angela asked.

"Maybe," T. J. mused. "Or maybe I'll do something to help people after they've had a stroke. Some sort of surgery that can make them the way they were before."

"Boy, my mom would love you," I blurted out. But as soon as the words were out of my mouth, I wished I could pull them back in. Because if I was right about all this, then my mom was T. J.'s mom too. And I could tell by the cloud that passed through T. J.'s eyes that she was thinking the same thing.

"What's she like?" T. J. asked, pulling her legs up under her on the chair. "Your mom, I mean."

"Well..." I looked at Angela. "How would you describe my mom?"

"She's a nurse," Angela said, giving me a jump start.

"That's right," I said. "She started out just working in the hospital. I don't know what she did. Then she went to night school and became a nurse's aide. Now she's a nurse."

"Yeah, but what's she *like?*" T. J. repeated. "I don't even remember what it's like to have a mom. Joe's great. He's really laid back and lots of fun. But sometimes he forgets important stuff like dentist appointments and school conferences. Of course, he doesn't think things like that are important. In some ways, he's like a big kid. He thinks the fun stuff is what really matters."

That was exactly how Mom described him.

"Sam's mom is definitely not a big kid," Angela said.

"Definitely not," I agreed. "In fact, she's probably the opposite of Joe. She's very serious and responsible. She doesn't know much about having fun."

"Oh, I don't know," Angela said. "She's gotten more fun since she and Bob decided to get married."

"Your mom's getting married?" T. J. asked.

Before I could answer, the front door burst open. We all shut up. "T. J.?" a man's voice called.

Sherlock scampered out from under T. J.'s chair and raced down the hall. "Woof! Woof!"

T. J. looked at me. "Joe's home."

"I figured."

"T. J.?" the voice called again. "Where are you? What's the big emergency?"

He poked his head into T. J.'s room and it was like everything stopped. He looked at me and I looked at him. And nobody said a word.

Chapter 17

If I ever had any doubt that this Joseph Wright was my father, that doubt was gone now. He was thinner than I expected. Shorter too. But other than that, he looked exactly like the photo T. J. had shown me. Exactly like the photo of him and my mom in those old newspaper articles too. Except he was older now.

He had the same white blond hair as me and T. J., a long face, and a full mustache. He wore an old white T-shirt that was spotted with flecks of paint and jeans that were so faded they were practically white.

This was my dad! I had waited for this moment for so long and now that it was here, I didn't know what to do. But I got the feeling he didn't know what to do, either.

T. J. broke the silence. "Joe, this is Sam and her friend, Angela. From Iowa." Her voice sounded funny. Like there was something caught in her throat. "Sam thinks you're her dad."

He still didn't say anything. He just stared at me. And I stared back.

"Joe?" T. J. said, her voice rising. Her knuckles were white from gripping the back of her desk chair so hard.

"H-how did you find us?" Joe asked me, his voice cracking.

I opened my mouth, but no words came out. I swallowed hard, then tried again. "A detective," I croaked. "On the internet."

Joe rubbed his face tiredly, as though he hadn't slept in days. "I don't suppose it was all that hard," he said finally. "I wouldn't have thought anyone was looking for me anymore, so these last few years I haven't exactly tried to hide."

"Hide?" T. J. asked. "W-why would you want to hide?"

Joe glanced around nervously. "Where's your mom?" he asked me.

"She's in Clearwater. She doesn't know I'm here."

His shoulders relaxed a little when I said that. But I couldn't tell what he thought about me being there in his house. Was he happy to see me or not?

"Sam says she had a sister," T. J. said. "She showed me a picture. She thinks I'm the sister she thought was dead. That's not...it's not true, is it?"

Joe rubbed the bridge of his nose between his eyebrows, then slumped against the doorjamb. A thousand questions swirled around in my head, but I couldn't grab one to ask. All I could do was stare wide-eyed at him—this man who was my dad.

"If it's true, then...you'd be my dad too," T. J. rose from her chair. There was panic in her eyes. "My *real* dad. But that's not right. My real dad died in a fire. You were my dad's best friend, right?"

He didn't answer.

"RIGHT?" she said again. Louder this time.

Joe let out a long sigh. "No, Teej," he said finally. "I...I am your real dad."

T. J.'s whole face went white.

"T. J. ..." Joe went over to her, but she backed away from him. "Let me explain."

"I can't deal with this." T. J. pushed past Joe and bolted out of her room. Sherlock dashed after her. A few seconds later we heard the front door open, then slam shut. Sherlock let out a soft whimper.

Joe cocked his head to the little rectangular window above. We could all hear T. J.'s heavy stomps across the yard.

"It's okay," Joe said nervously. "She's just going next door. She's got friends there. David and Nick. They're twins too." He smiled ruefully.

I didn't know what to say. I glanced at Angela. She looked as uncomfortable as I felt.

Joe rubbed his face again and smiled at me. "So... what do we do now?"

He was asking me? He was the grown-up here.

"Maybe we should go in the other room and talk," he suggested. "I don't know about you, but I sure could use something to drink."

"Okay," I said, slowly unfolding my legs.

"Um, I think I'll wait here," Angela said. She pulled out her phone. "I should call my dad and let him know where we are."

155.

Uh oh! We were going to miss that last bus back to Hill Valley! But...

"Do you want something to drink?" Joe asked Angela.

"No," she said, shaking her head. "I'm fine." She smiled nervously.

"Okay," he said. Then he turned and walked out of the room.

Angela gestured for me to go, so I hurried after him. Hopefully Angela and her dad would figure out how we would get back to Hill Valley.

My legs were so shaky I wasn't sure they'd hold me up. I did manage to find my dad, though. He was in a very small kitchen, standing in front of an open refrigerator door, his elbow resting on the top of the door. "Do you want a Coke?" he asked me.

"Okay." I tried to act casual, like this was no big deal, having a Coke with my dad.

He grabbed two cans from the fridge—a can of Coke and a can of beer—then plopped them both on the table. Wow! When he stood next to me, I could see I was almost as tall as he was.

I waited until he motioned for me to sit. Then I pulled out a chair and slowly eased myself into it. He sat down heavily in the chair beside me and we just sort of looked at each other. A ceiling fan hummed above us. For a moment, it was the only sound in the room.

"I don't know where to start," he said with a short laugh.

"Me either."

He shook his head. "Look at you. You're all grown up."

I blushed.

"Of course, T. J.'s grown up too, but that's different. I haven't watched you grow. Whenever I think of you, I still picture that three-year-old kid with the broken front tooth."

I did have a broken front tooth when I was a little kid. It happened when I fell off my tricycle.

"I never meant for it to be like this," he said, shifting in his seat. "I never thought...I never wanted..." His voice trailed off.

"Y-you took my sister," I said. It just popped out.

He looked down at his beer. "Yes."

But now that I'd started, I kept going. "You took her and you let everyone think she was *dead*." I didn't get it. This man sitting so close to me, *my dad,* seemed like a regular person. How could he have done this terrible thing?

"You have to understand, Sam. Your mom was taking the two of you away from me. She was heading off to medical school in Florida—"

Wait, what? "My mom never went to medical school." She'd be a doctor if she'd gone to medical school. Not a nurse.

"Well, that was her plan. Ever since I first met her, that was all she talked about. Becoming a doctor."

It was?

T. J. said she wanted to be a doctor. How bizarre was that?

"Then your mom got pregnant and we got married and I thought she'd given up all those big ideas," Joe said. "But she didn't. As soon as her folks moved down to Florida, they started telling her about this great medical school down there and how she could still go if she wanted to. They even offered to pay for it. They said they'd take care of you and T. J. while she was in class. All she had to do was move down there and everything would be set.

"So, one day she just up and decided this was what she was going to do. She went to see some hotshot lawyer. They wanted me to sign some paper that said it was okay if she took you two out of state. But it wasn't okay. It wasn't okay at all." He held his head in his hands.

"But..." I didn't even know where to begin with the questions. This was so totally different from anything I'd ever heard before. "I thought you guys got divorced because Sarah died."

Joe pressed his lips together. "Is that what your mother told you?"

"I think so." It was either her or Grandma Sperling. I wasn't sure who now.

"No." He shook his head vehemently. "Your mother wanted a divorce practically the day after we got married."

"She did? Why?"

But then I put it all together. They got married young. *Really* young. And Joe said she got pregnant and they got married. He didn't say they got married and *then* she got pregnant.

"My mom was pregnant before you guys got married?" I asked, totally shocked.

Hearing the words so bluntly seemed to shock Joe too. "Well," he hesitated. "Yeah. I guess that's the way it happened."

I couldn't believe it! My mom, Ms. Responsibility, got herself pregnant? Okay, but what did that have to do with why he took my sister? And he didn't just take her, he *faked her death*. That was worse than kidnapping. It was like...*murder* in a way. Sarah didn't really die, but we all thought she did. As far as we were concerned, she was dead.

"So, how did you..." I couldn't even say it out loud. I couldn't say *how did you fake my sister's death.*

"I never planned to take T. J. that day," he said. "It just...happened."

"How?" How did something like that just "happen?" And the other question that gnawed at the back of my brain: *Why did you only take her? Why didn't you take me too?*

He took another swallow of beer. "Like I said, your mom was taking you guys away. This was going to be my last chance to see either of you for quite a while. Maybe ever, if your grandparents had their way. So, I wanted to do something special. Just the three of us. Go on a picnic or something. But then you came down with the flu."

Yes! The family picnic. Except, I thought my mom was supposed to go on that too.

"I didn't think you were that sick," Joe went on. "I thought you could still come. I wasn't sure when I'd see you again! But your mom wouldn't hear of it. She let me take T. J., but not you. So, T. J. and me, we ended up at that old quarry outside Clearwater. She didn't know what was happening. She just ran up and down the path picking dandelions for your mom while my heart was breaking. All I could do was think about how unfair it was that your mom could take you both away from me, just like that."

"So, you decided to…make it look like Sarah died?" I asked, squeezing my hands around my Coke.

"No! I didn't want to take her back to your mom, but I never…I never thought about taking her away. Not at first. I just…I didn't know what to do. I drove her to my mother's. She was living in Waterloo then. She never thought it was right that your mom could take you both away. She wanted to help me. She said she'd keep T. J. for me and in the morning, I should call my lawyer and tell him I wasn't going to sign that paper.

"So, I drove back to Clearwater. But instead of going to your mom's, I drove back out to the quarry. I needed to figure out what I was going to say to your mom, how I was going to tell her T. J. wasn't coming home that night and that I wasn't going to let her take you guys to Florida. There was an old canoe lying in some brush. I don't know whose it was. You're not even supposed to go canoeing out there. But it was there, so I put it in the water and just sort of drifted around on the water for a while.

"A little while later, I heard voices. The sound startled me. It startled me so bad I dropped one of the oars. So, I jumped in after it. And then these people came running. They thought they saw a kid fall in.

"I don't know what I was thinking. It all happened so fast. I just sort of went along and said, 'Yes, my little girl fell in the water!' The lady went to get help and her husband tried to get me to come out of the water. But I wouldn't. I just kept diving under and coming back up. I don't know what I was doing.

"By the time the cops got there, I had done such a good job convincing these people that my kid really was in the water that I almost believed it myself.

"One of the cops found a kid's life preserver in the canoe. I didn't even know it was there. I told him Sarah had taken it off before she fell in. It was all so easy because everyone believed me. The fire department came out and started a search.

"Someone pulled me out of the water and dried me off. Pretty soon, your mom showed up. Those folks from that other car told the cops they saw a little girl fall into the water." He closed his eyes as though remembering was too painful. "Everyone kept yelling at me, telling me how stupid it was to take a little girl out in a canoe there. Like I didn't know that! People asked me whether I saw the No Swimming and No Boating signs. Your mom started pounding on my chest. I couldn't believe they all thought I was so stupid. That I would take a little girl out on that water. Let her take off her life preserver. But that was exactly what they thought. Every last one of them.

"Of course, my mother was all worked up too,"

Joe went on. "She didn't know what to do. This wasn't what we planned, but it was too late to go back. The story made news all over Iowa. And she had the kid that everyone was looking for. So, the first thing she did was tell everyone that T. J. was you. Then she told one of her friends that her other granddaughter was missing and that she had to come to Clearwater to be with the rest of the family. She asked the friend to take care of T. J. while she was gone. Told her T. J.'s name was Sam."

"What did you tell Sarah—er—T. J. about all of this?" I asked. "Didn't she think it was weird that she never got to go home again? Didn't she think it was weird that people were calling her Sam? And how did she become T. J.?"

"Well, she was only three years old. When we were calling her Sam, my mother told her it was just a funny game and she should pretend she was you. She always liked to play pretend. She stayed with my mother's friend until after the search was called off and we had the funeral. Then Mother thought I'd better get T. J.—er, Sarah—and disappear. Which was pretty easy because your mom wanted a divorce anyway. She was picking up and moving to Florida."

Except she never did.

Why not? Was she so broken up over losing one of her children that she couldn't move to Florida? She couldn't follow her dream of becoming a doctor?

"So what happened after that?" I asked.

"I told T. J. we were going on a little trip. Just her and

162

me. It was hard at first because she missed her mom and she especially missed you."

I smiled, then looked down at my can of pop. I liked that she'd missed me.

"There was a time she thought I called her Tara instead of Sarah and she thought that was another joke. She thought it was more pretend. So, I kept calling her Tara Jo instead of Sarah Jo. I realized it was probably a good idea to change her name anyway. Then Tara Jo got shortened to T. J.

"For the first couple of years, we just drove around the country. I told her you and your mom had died and we couldn't go back to Iowa. That we were going to have a whole new life. She didn't like it at first, but she got used to it. My mother sent us money now and then and told us what was going on. As far as the police were concerned, the case was closed. Sarah was dead.

"After a while, when I was sure no one was looking for T. J., we settled down in a small town in southern California. I got a job. Your sister started kindergarten. She started a year late because of all the moving around we did before that."

"That's why she's only going into eighth grade?"

"Yeah. We sort of skipped that first birthday, so when you guys turned five, she thought she was turning four.

"Then we moved to Oregon, then South Dakota, and finally Minnesota, because my mother had moved here. We moved in here with her. I found a guy who drew up some fake adoption papers a few years ago. He thought it was better to say T. J. was originally someone else's kid rather than mine. That way no one could trace her to Sarah.

"Once I got the adoption papers, I told T. J. she was adopted. I told her her real family died in a fire. I told her her dad and I were real close. She didn't question it. She doesn't remember much about her life in Clearwater."

"She doesn't remember me," I said, picking at the tab on my can of Coke. "She said she once had a brother named Sam, but she doesn't remember ever having a sister."

"There was a boy in California she used to play with. His name was Sam too. Somewhere along the way I think she confused the two of you, and I guess I thought that was okay."

I closed my eyes. Maybe when I opened them I'd find out this whole thing was just a dream. A bad dream.

Unfortunately, it was all real.

"I never stopped thinking about you, Sam," Joe said, his elbows on the table, leaning toward me. It was what I'd always wanted to hear. "I knew I could never go looking for you. But I always hoped you'd come looking for me. I just didn't expect you to come looking so soon. And I never figured out what I'd do if you found me."

"That's why you didn't call me back last week?"

"When I heard that message on the machine, I wanted to take T. J. and run again. But I couldn't do that. My mom—your Grandma Wright—she's pretty sick. She's

164

had a couple of strokes and she can't take care of herself anymore, so she's in a nursing home. T. J. and me, we're all she has left. She was always there for us, so now it's our turn to be there for her."

I didn't know what to think of this grandmother who had not only abandoned me my whole life, but had helped my dad take T. J. away from us. This grandmother who was probably too sick to explain to me why she'd done it.

"I had our number changed," Joe went on. "Got it unlisted and hoped that would be enough. After all, it wasn't Suzanne who'd found me, it was you. If you were the one looking for me instead of your mom, I thought maybe you'd just give up. But I bet you're like your mom. You probably never give up."

I couldn't think of many people who would describe me like that.

"I'm nothing like my mom." I always thought I was like him. Casual. Loose. A go-with-the-flow sort of person. But I was different than he was. Very different. I couldn't imagine ever doing what he'd done.

"So, what do we do now?" Joe asked. He looked like an old man and a little kid at the same time.

"I-I don't know." We had to tell my mom. That's what we had to do now.

He slapped his hand down on the kitchen table. "Well, to start with, I guess I should go and get T. J. When we get back, we'll have some supper and then figure out what to do next, okay?"

I nodded. I didn't have a clue what to say. My head was spinning.

Joe squeezed my shoulder and I felt an electric current go right through my skin. It was the first time in ten whole years my dad had touched me. But it was over almost as soon as it began.

"Don't go anywhere," he said as he yanked open the front door. "I'll be back in a minute."

Chapter 18

I'm not sure how long I sat there at the kitchen table, trying to make sense of everything I'd just heard.

I was so confused. I knew I should probably hate my dad for what he'd done. Thinking about what he did, what he had stolen from Mom and Grandma and Grandpa Sperling and me…it made me feel sick. But I didn't hate him. I wasn't sure what I felt for him, but it wasn't hatred.

Then I thought about my mom. What would she do when she found out? She'd have my dad thrown in jail. That much I knew for sure. What he did was a *crime,* right?

T. J. would come live with us and my dad would go to jail and that would be the end of it.

All of a sudden, their dog let out a shrill *woof!* His tags jangled as he got up on his hind legs, paws on the front windowsill, tail wagging, and peered out the window.

Were they back?

I got up from the table and went to look outside. Joe and T. J. were sitting on the grass under the big tree out front. Joe had his arm around T. J. and she had her head resting on his shoulder. Their backs were to me, but because the windows were open I could hear every word they were saying.

"What are we going to do?" T. J. moaned.

"I don't know, honey."

"Will…her mom take me away from you?"

"She'll sure want to try."

T. J.'s shoulders quivered and Joe hugged her tighter to him. "But I want to stay with you," she said. "Can't we run away or something?"

I gasped. T. J. would rather run away with…Joe, who was a liar and a *criminal,* than come live with us?

"No," he said. He sounded tired. "No more running."

"I wish she'd never come here!" T. J. cried. Each word she spoke was like a fist in my stomach.

"I wish—"

I didn't hang around to hear what else T. J. wished. I hustled back to T. J.'s bedroom, where I figured I'd find Angela waiting. New plan: we were going to sneak out the back door right now, cut across the yards, and be out of here before my dad and T. J. came back. I'd just suck this whole thing up inside me and pretend it never happened. I'd go back home and take whatever punishment my mom wanted to dole out for sneaking off to Minnesota without permission, for sneaking off to the Twin Cities without permission. I'd tell her I didn't know what got into me. I just felt like doing something reckless.

But Angela wasn't in the bedroom.

"Angela?" I called, looking all around.

"In here," she called from a closed door behind me. The bathroom. "I'll be out in a minute."

I sighed, leaning my head against the wall. What was I thinking coming here?

I heard a toilet flush and the water come on. Finally, Angela opened the door. "Hey," she said softly. "How'd it go?"

"Fine," I said, grabbing her arm. "But we've got to get out of here. Come on."

"Wait." Angela dug in her heels. "What's the matter, Sam? What happened?"

"This was a mistake," I said. "A huge mistake." I told her a little bit about what my dad had told me and then I told her everything I'd overheard between my dad and T. J.

"I never realized what a mess of things I'd make by coming here," I said. "If my mom finds out about this, my dad will go to jail. And then T. J. will have to come live with us and...she doesn't want to." My throat closed up and my eyes filled with tears. My bottom lip quivered. "Sh-she doesn't even know us, but she doesn't want to live with us." I buried my face in my hands and just let the tears come.

Angela put her arms around me. "Shh," she said, rubbing my back. "I have to tell you, Sam, I think I understand how she feels. What if some stranger came along and told you your mom had done something wrong and now you had to go live with him? How would you feel?"

I wiped my tears on the back of my arm and sniffed.

"But I'm not some stranger. I'm her *sister*. Her twin sister."

"You're a stranger to her," Angela said.

She was right, of course. And in that instant, I realized that Joe and T. J. were a family, but they weren't *my* family. They were my blood relatives, but they were no more my family than Bob's family was.

I sniffed again. "That's why we have to leave. Now. Before they come back inside."

"No, Sam! You can't just pretend this whole thing never happened. What about your mom? Don't you think she has a right to know the truth?"

Yes, she did. And T. J. and my dad had a right to…to what? I didn't know. I had screwed things up by coming here, and now I didn't know where my loyalties lay. All I knew was I didn't want to be the one responsible for sending my dad to jail. And I didn't want to be the one responsible for ruining everyone's life.

"There's something else you need to know, Sam," Angela said. As if I hadn't already found out enough.

"What?" I asked, slumping against the wall.

"I…talked to your mom—"

"What?" I cried, panic rising in my throat.

Angela led me back to T. J.'s room and we sat back down on her bed. "When I called my dad's house, Noreen answered the phone," Angela explained. "She wanted to know where I was. And then she wanted to know whether you were with me. Your mom was there, Sam. She was at my dad's house. She drove up to Hill Valley as soon as she got your message this morning."

Oh no. "What did you tell her?"

"I didn't tell her anything," Angela assured me. "Not about your dad or T. J. You're the one who should tell her about that. I told her we went to the Mall of America, which we did, right? She wanted to talk to you, but I told her you were in the bathroom. I've told her that three times now because she keeps calling back. She probably thinks you're sick or something. You probably better call her."

"No!" I couldn't talk to my mom. Not yet. What would I say?

"Sam, you have to! She knows something's up, but she doesn't know what. And she and my dad are both on their way to the Mall of America to get us. We're supposed to meet them in front of Bloomingdale's in an hour."

"An hour?" I screeched.

Angela nodded miserably. "You've got to call her and tell her where we are."

Or...we could sneak out like I just said, run through the backyards, cut over to Penn Avenue and catch a bus to the Mall of America. We might even get there before my mom and Angela's dad. The only thing we'd have to tell them was we felt like sneaking off for a day of fun at the Mall of America. We're teenagers. Teenagers do stuff like that.

No. Angela was right. I had to call my mom and tell her the truth. She deserved to know.

I dragged myself to my feet, then tottered over to the window. My dad and T. J. were still out there. I couldn't hear them as well here as I could in the living room, but I didn't want to take any chances on them hearing me. So, I went into the bathroom and turned on the shower to drown out my voice.

"You're doing the right thing," Angela called over the noise of the water.

I hoped she was right.

I sat down on the toilet seat, opened my purse and took out my phone. My whole body was shaking. But one by one I punched in each digit of my mom's number.

What was I going to say?

Mom picked up on the first ring. "Hello? Sam?"

I gulped. It was so good to hear her voice. "Uh huh."

"Oh, thank God! Do you have any idea, any idea at all, what I've been going through these last twenty-four hours?"

Probably nothing in comparison to what she was about to go through.

"I tell you, Sam, I don't know what goes through your head anymore. I specifically told you to get on that bus this morning and come home, and what do you do? You hop on another bus and take off for the Mall of America? Do you have any idea how dangerous that is?"

"Well—" I began.

"No, you probably don't," Mom went on, her voice rising. If I wasn't careful, I was going to start crying again. "Because you're thirteen and you think you know it all! You think you can do whatever you want. Well, let me tell you something, Sam. There are going to be some

changes around here when we get back to Clearwater.
Some big changes."

"I'll say," I muttered.

"Are you being fresh with me, young lady?"

"No!" I said right away. Because I really wasn't being
fresh. Not this time.

I took a deep breath. "I've got something to tell you,
Mom."

"What? What do you have to tell me?"

I glanced over at the stream of water pouring from the
faucet and swirling down the drain.

This was so hard.

"Well," I said weakly. "First I think you'd better pull
over. I don't think you should be driving when I say what
I have to say—"

"Do you really think I'm driving right now, Samantha?"
Mom yelled. *"I am way too upset to be driving!"*

"Oh. Good," I said, relieved. "I mean, good that you're
not driving." This was going to come as a huge shock and
I didn't want her to drive off the road or anything.

Mom sighed. "What is it, Sam?"

I swallowed again. I wished I could be a little kid
again and have her put her arms around me and tell me
everything was going to be okay.

"Sam?" Mom said, more worried this time.

There was no easy way to say it, so I just opened my
mouth and blurted out, "I found my dad and I'm at his
house and T. J., I mean Sarah, is here too. She's alive, just
like I thought. And...she's living with him, and..." And I

had to stop there because I was out of breath.

But I'd said it.

There was a long pause. Then, "W-what did you say?" Mom asked in a voice barely louder than a whisper.

I closed my eyes and leaned back against the toilet seat. Did I really have to say it all over again?

"I said, 'I found my dad and—'"

"Sarah's...alive?" Mom interrupted.

"Yes!"

"She's there with you?"

"Well, not right here. She's outside. With him. She didn't know anything about you and me. She thought—well, never mind right now. They're out there talking and then—"

"Where are you right now?" Mom wanted to know.

"I told you, I'm at...my dad's house."

"Yes, but where is that? What's the address?"

I told her.

"You stay put," Mom demanded. "I'm calling the police. I'll be there as soon as I can."

"Wait, Mom! Don't call the police," I begged. What would my dad and T. J. think when the police pulled up in their driveway?

But it was too late. Mom had already hung up.

Chapter 19

I heard the sirens less than five minutes later. Silently, Angela and I made our way to the front door. As soon as we stepped outside we saw three police cars pulling up in front of the house.

Joe and T. J. both scrambled to their feet. T. J. turned to me and I saw a look of horror creep across her face.

"You called the police?" she cried.

Joe's shoulders slumped. He looked at me with sadness in his eyes.

"No! I just...called my mom—"

"Oh. So *she* called the police," T. J. said in a nasty voice. Which made me kind of mad. I mean, I didn't want my mom to call the police, but I understood why she did. What Joe did was *wrong*. Didn't T. J. see that?

Losing my sister was so painful for my mom that even now, ten years later, she could hardly talk about it. And all along, Sarah—T. J.—was never really dead. It seemed to me that telling people someone was dead when they weren't was one of the worst things a person could do.

I don't know whether I could've said that to T. J.

or not, but I didn't even have a chance to try because all those police officers were getting out of their cars and marching over to us. There were six of them—two from each vehicle. A tall female officer told us her name was Detective Becker and she wanted to know which of us girls was Samantha Wright. There was something a little bit freaky about hearing your name come out of a policewoman's mouth. I swallowed hard, then slowly raised my hand.

Then they wanted to know whether my dad was Joseph Wright and whether T. J. was Sarah Wright.

"My name's not Sarah," T. J. said boldly. "It's T. J."

"What's your mother's name, T. J.?" another officer asked.

"I don't have a mother. My mother died when I was little."

"What was her name?" he pressed.

T. J. lowered her eyes. She drew closer to Joe and he hugged her against his chest. I looked away. Neighbors were starting to come out of their houses to see what was going on.

"T. J.?" Detective Becker tried to get T. J. to look at her and answer the question, but T.J. just buried her face in my dad's chest.

So, the police decided to haul all of us down to the police station.

"You can't do that!" Angela said. "Our parents are picking us up at the Mall of America. They're going to wonder where we are."

"No, I spoke with Samantha's mother, and all of your parents are planning on picking you up at the police station," Detective Becker explained.

I was surprised how relieved I was to hear that. This whole thing was getting to be too much for me to handle. Way too much. I wanted my mom. And I was willing to let the police take me to her.

But T. J. didn't want to get into that police car for anything. Especially when they told her she was going to ride in one car and Joe was going to ride in another.

"No!" T. J. screamed, wide-eyed. She wrapped her entire body around Joe and held on for dear life.

"Please don't make me go!" she cried. "Please!" Tears poured down her face.

Joe was crying too. His shoulders were heaving and he was clinging to T. J. every bit as hard as she was clinging to him.

It took four police officers to wrestle the two of them apart and drag them into separate vehicles, T. J. kicking and screaming, and Joe crying the entire time.

I could hardly bear to watch. This was my sister and my dad. They were in so much pain. And it was all my fault. Well, it was my dad's fault, too, but mostly it was mine. Because I was the one who couldn't leave well enough alone.

Detective Becker led Angela and me to the first vehicle. "You girls can ride with us," she said.

We crawled into the backseat of the car. I'd never been in a police car before. It smelled bad. Like stale cigarette smoke and cheeseburgers.

There was a glass panel separating the front and back seats, but the officers kept the panel open so they could talk to us. Maybe they thought we'd feel better if they drove the speed limit and made conversation with us. But the only thing that would make me feel better was if I could go home.

The heavyset guy who was driving had a daughter our age, he told us. She was a swimmer, and I don't remember what else because I wasn't really listening. I just leaned against the window and watched the city go by. I wondered how T. J. was doing in the car behind ours.

When we got to the police station, the officers took us all to separate rooms. They even separated me and Angela. The heavyset guy took Angela into one conference room and Detective Becker took me into another one across the hall. She flipped a switch and an overhead fluorescent light blinked on.

Detective Becker gestured for me sit down on one of the three chairs surrounding the hard metal table in the middle of the room. There was nothing else in the entire room besides the table and chairs. No books or magazines. Even the walls were bare. No pictures. No clock. No outside window. Just a window to the hallway and there were blinds covering that.

I chose the closest chair and Detective Becker sat down across from me.

"Sounds like you've had quite a day," she began. "Do you want to tell me about it?"

There was a lot more to tell about than just today, so,

once again, I started at the beginning. I told about my visit to the psychic, the newspaper articles, this feeling I had that my sister was still alive and how I went about trying to find out for sure. I told about how I wasn't supposed to go to Hill Valley with Angela, but that I went anyway, and how this morning I was supposed to get on a bus in Hill Valley and go back home, but instead I took a bus to the Mall of America, and everything that happened after that.

Every now and then Detective Becker wrote something down in her spiral notebook, but mostly she just listened. When I finished, we went over it all again so she could make sure she got everything right. Finally, she stood up and said she was going to go check on everyone else. And then I was alone.

I wondered what was going to happen now. They'd probably want to talk to my mom, too, when she got here. Was she here already? Was she in one of the other rooms? What about Angela? Was she still here?

I opened the door and poked my head out. Angela and her dad were just coming out of the room across the hall. Which meant my mom was probably here somewhere too.

"Samantha, hi," Mr. Hunter said all friendly-like, as though we weren't all standing in the middle of a police station.

"Hey, Sam," Angela scurried over and grabbed my hand. "How are you?"

"Okay. Do you know where my mom is?" I asked.

Angela shook her head.

"She and that fellow she came up here with were talking with the police when I got here," Mr. Hunter said.

"Fellow she came up here with?" I raised an eyebrow.

"Yes, the fiancé from Iowa—"

Bob? Bob was here too?

"They drove their own vehicle," Mr. Hunter continued. "Which was probably a good thing. Sounds like you're all going to be here a while."

I didn't know why my mom had to go and drag Bob along. It wasn't like they were married yet.

"Are you ready to go, Angela?" Mr. Hunter asked.

"In a minute. I just want to say good-bye to Sam first."

Mr. Hunter moved down the hall to give us a little privacy. Once he was far enough away so he couldn't hear, Angela leaned toward me. "Guess what?" she whispered.

"What?"

"My dad thought something bad had happened to us. He was actually *worried.*" She seemed really happy about that.

When I didn't say anything, she said, "Don't you get it? That means *he cares about me.* He even gave me a hug when he saw me. A real hug!"

I smiled. "That's nice, Angela."

"Looks like there's hope for my dad after all. And if there's hope for him, maybe there's hope for your situation too."

It was weird listening to Angela talk about hope. At the moment, I wasn't sure I'd ever feel hopeful about anything again.

We said our good-byes, then Angela and her dad left. I peered up and down the hallway, wondering where my mom was. Leaving the door slightly ajar, I went back to the table to wait.

I took out my comb and mindlessly ran it through my hair for something to do. What was happening in all those other rooms? Were my mom and Joe and T. J. giving their own versions of what happened? Were they arresting Joe? Getting T. J. ready to come live with us?

About the time I was starting to think I'd been forgotten, there was a light tapping at my door. I looked up.

"Hey there, Sam," Bob said. He had my suitcase in one hand and a paper bag from McDonald's in the other. He walked in and set the suitcase on the floor and the McDonald's bag on the table. Then he leaned over and wrapped his big arms around me.

I just sort of melted into him. Wow. Bob and I had never hugged before. But…it felt okay. Good, even.

"How are you?" he asked. There was so much concern on his face that my eyes filled with tears.

"I'll bet you're hungry," he said. I could smell the hamburger and fries on the table beside me. And then I realized that yes, I was indeed hungry.

"Quarter pounder with cheese, no pickles, right?" Bob asked.

"Yes," I said, surprised that he knew I didn't like pickles.

"So, what's going on?" I asked as we sat down at the table and dug into the food. "Where's my mom?"

"Well," Bob said. She's talking to some people about what it would take to try and get temporary custody of T. J. tonight, but I don't think she's going to be successful."

"Why not?" I asked, my mouth full of cheeseburger.

"Because this is a very complicated case. It's going to take a while for a judge to talk to everyone and decide what's in the best interests of the child."

"What's complicated about it? My dad committed a crime."

"Yes and no," Bob said. "I'm not sure he can really be charged with a crime because at the time he took your sister, there was no divorce. No custody agreement. He had the same rights to you and your sister that your mom had."

What? I swallowed the food in my mouth. "He had a right to tell everyone she was dead and then take her away?" I exclaimed. "That's kidnapping! And—" I didn't know what else it was. Not exactly murder, but there had to be a name for what he did.

"Not as far as the law is concerned," Bob said. "That's why I'm saying it's complicated."

"But…he lied to the police. He made everyone search the quarry. All for nothing. Isn't that a crime?"

"Well, yes," Bob admitted. "But honestly, we're not likely to do anything about it now. Not after all this time. The real issue here is your sister and what's in her best interest." I'd forgotten for a second that Bob wasn't just my mom's fiancé. He was a cop too. Just like Detective Becker and all these other people here.

I picked at my French fries. "So, you don't think Joe will go to jail?" I asked.

"I don't think so. The main issue here is going to be custody. And that'll have to be hashed out in court. The thing is, your sister has been with your dad for ten years. She wants to stay with him. The judge is going to factor that in."

"Have my mom and T. J. seen each other yet?"

"Yes," Bob said. "But it doesn't sound like the meeting went very well. Emotions are running pretty high right now. On both sides. This is going to take some time."

"Well, if my mom doesn't get custody of T. J. tonight, what will happen to T. J.? Where will she go?"

"I suspect she'll go into temporary foster care."

Foster care? My heart ached. In foster care, T. J. really would be with strangers.

I suddenly wasn't hungry anymore. "I shouldn't have done this," I said, pushing my half-eaten cheeseburger away. "I shouldn't have gone looking for my dad."

Bob didn't answer right away. "I understand why you did."

I raised my eyes. The main reason I went looking for my dad was I wanted to know what he thought of somebody else adopting me. I wanted him to put his foot down and say no, he didn't want anyone else to adopt me. That he was my dad. How could Bob possibly understand when he was the "someone else" who wanted to adopt me?

Bob scooted his chair forward a little. "I lost my dad

when I was right around your age, Sam. I know what it's like to grow up without a father."

"Your dad got shot on duty, right?" I said slowly. I was pretty sure that was what my mom had said.

"Yes. During a convenience store robbery." Bob had a faraway look in his eyes. "He wasn't the kind of father who spent a lot of time with his kids. He put in a long day at work, came home, and relaxed in front of the television. He was right there in our living room every single night, but I didn't know him. Not really. I didn't know who he was, what he thought about, what he was like as a kid. I didn't even know for sure that he loved me."

It was weird to think of Bob as a thirteen-year-old kid who just wanted a little love and attention from his dad. Like me.

"When he died," Bob went on, "I realized I'd never know those things. But it was different for you. You never knew for sure your dad was really gone. You still had a chance to get to know him. That's why you went looking for him. Even though you knew it would hurt your mom."

I swallowed hard. "I never meant to hurt my mom." I never meant to hurt *anybody*. "I just—" How could I justify this?

"You just wanted to know whether your dad could ever love you."

I nodded. Maybe Bob did understand.

"You know, you and I will never be blood relatives." Bob leaned a little closer to me and looked right into my eyes. "But we can still be a family."

I knew that was all he and my mom wanted. For us to be a family. The funny thing was I had been looking for a family too. Just not the same family my mom and Bob had been looking for. Maybe that was my mistake.

"D-do you have to adopt me for us to be a family?" I asked. I don't know where I got the guts to come right out and ask that question. But that was what it came down to for me. I had nothing against Bob. I just didn't want him to adopt me.

If Bob was upset or hurt, he didn't show it. "A piece of paper doesn't make us a family," he said. "Sometimes, family is a choice, not an obligation."

I'd never thought of it that way before. I always knew you could choose your friends, but I never thought about whether or not you could ever choose your family. Sometimes you *could* choose your family.

* * *

I yawned. It seemed like Bob and I had been stuck in that little conference room forever. I'd lost track of how many games of hangman we'd played. But we didn't have room on the McDonald's bag for any more games. That was how long we'd been there. I checked my phone. It was almost nine o'clock.

"You getting tired?" Bob asked.

"Yeah, a little," I said. I was getting hungry too. I wished I hadn't thrown away half of my cheeseburger.

Bob must have read my mind. He reached into his back pocket and pulled out his wallet. "There's probably a vending machine out there somewhere. Why don't you go get a little snack."

"Okay," I said.

Bob waved a five-dollar bill at me.

"Oh, that's okay. I've got money," I said, patting my purse.

Bob pushed the bill across the table. "Take it," he said. "And while you're at it, bring me some M&M's."

"Okay." I was really in the mood for a bag of M&M's myself. "Thanks."

I went out in the hall. If I went to the left, I knew I'd come out by the front door. I didn't remember seeing a vending machine anywhere that direction, so I went the other way.

The hallway ended at a small waiting room. Two chairs sat on either side of a square table that was piled with magazines. Across the room was a vending machine.

I stopped. T. J. stood in front of the machine dropping coins into the slot.

"I-I didn't know you were still here," I said.

She whirled around when she heard my voice, then slowly turned back to the machine. "I'm waiting for the lady from the Department of Human Services to show up." T. J. pressed a button and her candy dropped to the tray at the bottom.

M&M's.

I leaned against the wall. "My mom's...*fiancé* sent me

down here to get us some candy," I said stupidly.

I didn't want her to think I was copying her, so I said, "He wanted some M&M's. I don't know what I'm going to get for myself."

T. J. walked around me without looking at me, then sank down in one of the square chairs. I watched as she ripped open her bag of M&M's.

I didn't know what to do. Should I get what I came here to get and go back to the conference room? Or should I sit down next to T. J.?

I took a good hard look at her, this girl who was my sister. Her eyes drooped and her face was all blotchy like she'd been crying. Her whole life had just been turned upside down. And it was all my fault. She must really hate me.

"You probably hate me," T. J. said suddenly.

"What?" Why would I hate her? "I thought *you* hated *me.*"

T. J. blinked. "I don't even know you."

I sat down in the chair next to her, resting one foot under my butt. "I don't know you, either." And I *wanted* to know her. I wanted to know her even more than I wanted to know my dad.

T. J. popped an M&M into her mouth, then offered the bag to me. I shook five candies into my hand, then gave the bag back.

Silence.

"It's not that I don't want to get to know you or your mother," T. J. said after a little while. It sounded weird when she said "your mother." Like my mother wasn't her mother too. "I just…"

"You don't want to come live with us."

She shook her head and looked down at her lap. "I don't want to leave Joe. Or my grandma."

My throat caught when she said that. Her grandma was my grandma too. And I didn't even know her.

"But Joe took you away from us," I said. What he did was wrong.

She shrugged. "He's still my dad. Nothing he did all those years ago changes that. And now your mom wants to take me away from him."

Of course, she does. *After what your dad did, why shouldn't she take you away from him?*

"What if it was you?" T. J. asked. "What if you were going on about your life, not knowing anything about me or Joe. And one day Joe just sort of popped into your life and said your mom did something bad and now you have to come live with us. Would you want to?"

I always thought that if my dad ever came into my life and asked me to come live with him, I'd go in a second. I wouldn't even look back. But would I really? Mom and I didn't always get along, but she was my mom. She was the only parent I'd had. Would I really leave her and go live with some stranger even if he was my dad?

"I don't know," I said truthfully. Maybe I wouldn't.

"I'm still getting used to the idea that I have a mom and a sister. Just because somebody says it's true doesn't make it true. Do you know what I mean?"

I thought about what Bob had said about how a piece of paper doesn't make you family.

I understood T. J.'s point, but still. What about my mom? She wanted her daughter back. Didn't she deserve to have her daughter back?

How would we ever resolve this? There were no right answers. There weren't even any okay answers. No matter what happened, nobody was going to come out of this totally happy.

Chapter 20

It was dark outside when we finally left the police station. Bob drove over to a Holiday Inn that was just down the street and he and my mom paid for two adjoining rooms. One for my mom and me. And one for Bob.

I had my suitcase, but neither of them had an overnight bag. They weren't planning on staying overnight when they left Clearwater this morning. They thought they'd just pick me up in Hill Valley, then turn around and go back home.

"Should we see if we can find a Walmart or someplace where we can get a change of clothes or at least a couple of toothbrushes?" Bob asked as we trudged down the carpeted hallway, looking for our rooms.

"No," Mom said. "I'm tired. We can get something in the morning."

We stopped in front of room 235 and Bob inserted the plastic card in the slot and opened the door. I walked in and plopped my suitcase on one of the beds. Mom slowly sat down on the edge of the other bed. Bob unlocked the adjoining door between our rooms and went over to check out his room.

"I still think there's something screwy going on here," Mom called to Bob. "Why can't I take Sarah home tonight?"

"T. J.," I corrected. But no one paid any attention to me.

Bob walked back into our room. "Honey, you know why," he said, sitting down with my mom. "A judge is going to have to hear testimony—"

"But why?" My mom sprang to her feet. "She's my daughter! He took my daughter away! And now if she says she wants to stay with him, I may never get her back? It's not right!"

"No, it's not," Bob agreed.

"There's got to be something we can get him on," she said, stomping around the room. "Falsifying documents? Deprivation of parental rights? Whether we were divorced or not, you can't tell me that what he did was legal." She glared at Bob as though daring him to contradict her.

"Well—"

My mom cut him off. "What about all the money the county spent on dragging the quarry, looking for Sarah's body all those years ago? Maybe the county can bring charges against him."

"Oh, that'll really make T. J. want to come live with us," I mumbled. "If you find a way to get Joe arrested."

"Sam," Bob said in a warning voice.

Mom whirled around to face me. Her eyes were angry little slits. "Don't call her T. J. Her name is Sarah," she said firmly.

"No, it's not!" I stood tall. "Sarah is dead. The girl we knew as Sarah is gone. She's never coming back. This girl's name is T. J. We have to call her T. J."

As far as I was concerned, Sarah and T. J. were two totally different people. Sarah was the girl I used to play Barbies with. The girl I once shared a room with. The girl I would've shared all my secrets with, if things had been different.

I had no idea who T. J. was. I just knew she wasn't Sarah.

"Your sister's name is Sarah," Mom insisted. We stood eye to eye. Nose to nose. We were so close to one another that I could feel her angry breath on my face. And she could feel mine.

"Do you really think she's going to want to go back to being called Sarah when she's been T. J. for ten years?" I cried. "Geez, why don't you ever think about what other people want? Do you really think you can control everyone and everything?"

My mom looked like she'd been slapped. But I was just getting warmed up.

I think Bob could tell, too, because he stood up and put his hand on my shoulder. "Now, take it easy there, Sam," he said.

But I couldn't take it easy. I needed to tell my mother how I really felt about some things.

"It's not just T. J., you know. You do this with me too. You try and control my entire life!"

Mom gasped. "I'm your mother! I'm allowed to control your life."

"You shouldn't be allowed to control everything. Did you ever think maybe I needed to know stuff about my dad and my sister? Maybe I don't want to move out of my house and go live in a brand-new house! Maybe I don't want Bob to adopt me!"

Mom pressed her lips together. "Okay, Sam. That's enough—"

"You're doing it again!" I stomped my foot. "I'm not done talking, but you're still trying to control how much I say!"

I took a deep breath and tried to lower my voice. "Bob and I talked about him adopting me while you were doing whatever it was you were doing at the police station. I told him I wasn't sure I wanted him to adopt me, and do you know what? He's fine with it! You're probably the only one who's going to have a problem with it."

Mom sank to the bed. But I still wasn't done.

"Haven't you ever heard the phrase: 'If you love something, set it free'? 'If it comes back to you, it's yours. If it doesn't, it never was.' Mom, did it ever occur to you that maybe people don't belong to each other? I don't belong to you! And T. J. doesn't belong to you! If you push this thing with her, you're going to lose her forever! Is that what you want?"

"Whoa!" Bob said, stepping in between the two of us. He made a T with his hands. "Time out. I think the two of you need a break from this conversation. Sam, it's late. Why don't you go to bed."

What? *He* was telling me when to go to bed?

"And Suzanne..." I realized right then that my mom wasn't even *looking* at me. "Why don't you come over to my room and we can talk without disturbing Sam."

My mom just stared. She looked like a zombie sitting there and I started to feel a pain in my chest. Maybe I had gone too far? Or...maybe Bob was right and Mom and I needed a break from this conversation. I was pretty tired.

"Okay, I'll go to bed," I said. I moved my suitcase so I could pull back my covers.

Bob took my mom's hand and pulled her back up. Then he slowly walked her across the room.

"Good night, Mom," I said quietly. "Good night... Bob."

"Good night, honey," Bob said.

My mom didn't say anything. I wonder if she even heard me.

* * *

I didn't get a lot of sleep that night. I don't think my mom or Bob did, either. All night long I heard muffled voices coming from next door. Sometimes I even heard crying. I didn't think my mom ever cried.

At some point, I fell asleep. And obviously my mom must have come back because when I woke up the next morning she was sound asleep in the other bed, her back to me. The door between our room and Bob's was open and I could hear him snoring.

I closed my eyes and tried to go back to sleep, but I

couldn't. I was too wired to sleep. What was going to happen today?

A few minutes later I heard my mom roll over. I opened one eye and glanced over at her. She was awake too.

"Good morning," she said.

I swallowed hard. "Good morning," I said back.

Mom sat up. "I think you and I need to finish our conversation from last night," she said. She sounded a lot calmer this morning.

I was calmer too. "Okay," I said, pulling my sheet up to my chin.

Mom got up and came over to sit next to me on my bed. I shifted over to make room for her.

"Sam, do you like Bob? Are you okay about us getting married?"

"I like him," I said, gazing up at the sprinkler on the ceiling. "And it's okay that you're getting married." Really, it was. "It's just…it's going to be different having him in our family, being part of his family, having him live with us."

"Yes, it will," Mom agreed. She smiled. "But it'll be a good kind of different, don't you think? Bob's a wonderful man. And he loves you as much as he loves me. Believe me, I wouldn't marry anyone who didn't. He wants to be a father to you, Sam."

"I know." I propped myself up on my elbow. "But Mom, it doesn't matter how wonderful Bob is. I still have another father out there. I know I shouldn't have gone looking for him behind your back. But I just had to know something about him."

"Now you probably know more than you wish you did."

I nodded. "I'm sorry, Mom."

"Me too, honey." Mom leaned over and hugged me. "I wish I had tried harder to find him when you first started asking questions. I guess I figured once Bob and I were married, he would be all the father you'd ever need. That's why I wanted him to adopt you. But if that's not what you want, it's fine. He and I talked about that last night. He doesn't have to adopt you if you don't want him to."

"I don't know what I want," I said honestly. "I just know there's this hole inside me and I don't know what can fill it. I've known all along that Bob can't fill it. But I don't think that…Joe can fill it, either. Maybe I need… both Bob and Joe to fill it." I raised my eyebrow, trying to gauge my mom's reaction to that.

She only flinched a little. "I know you'd like to get to know your dad now."

I *thought* I wanted to get to know him. I was still pretty confused about all this.

"I understand that, Sam," Mom said. "Really, I do." She reached for my hand. "It'll take some time, but eventually I'll be at a place where that will be okay."

"Really?" I asked, surprised.

Mom nodded. "As long as you promise to try and be part of your other new family too. The family that includes Bob and his mother and brother and sisters."

"I can do that," I said. If she could give me the freedom to get to know my dad at some point, then I would do anything for her in return.

Mom scooted back on my bed and leaned against the headboard. "I think the hardest piece of this puzzle is going to be T. J.," she said with a heavy sigh.

I sat up. "Y-you called her T. J.!"

"Yeah," Mom said softly. She put an arm around me. "You were right about that last night."

Mom rested her head against mine. "She goes by T. J. now. We can't go back to calling her Sarah. And if she doesn't want to come live with us, we can't force her to or we'll lose her forever. Just like you said."

"S-so you're not going to try and get custody right now?" I asked.

Mom shook her head. "Bob and I were up most of the night talking about this. Much as I'd like to go over there and demand that T. J. come live with us and Joe go to jail…it just wouldn't be right, would it?"

I looked away. "No," I said sadly.

"If she's happy, he must have done something right during these ten years," Mom said.

For a while, neither of us said anything. Then I asked, "Are you glad we found out the truth? Or do you wish we hadn't?"

At first Mom didn't say anything. I could see her weighing it all out in the expressions that passed across her face. Finally, she cupped her hand around my chin and smiled. "I think it's always better to know the truth."

"Me too," I said. And then we just hugged each other until Bob came over and asked if it was time for breakfast.

Chapter 21

"Hurry up, Sam!" Mom called from our front door. "We don't want to be late!"

"I'm coming!" I called back. I fluffed my hair a couple more times, then peered at myself in my mirror. My hair wasn't perfect, but it would have to do.

I grabbed my purse, then hurried down the hall, weaving through all the boxes. My mom and Bob were getting married in three days. The movers were coming in four days. Grandma and Grandpa Sperling were coming tomorrow. And my sister, T. J., was coming today! I checked the clock on my phone. My mom and I had exactly one hour to drive to the Cedar Rapids bus station to meet her bus.

"Do I look okay?" I asked my mom, spinning around for her inspection. I had on a brand-new white blouse, my favorite jeans, and a gold monkey necklace.

"You look fine," Mom said. "How do I look?" She was wearing a blue skirt and a button-down white shirt.

"Fine," I said.

Then we went out to the car. We figured that since

this was T. J.'s first visit, Mom and I should go to the bus station to get her alone. T. J. could see Bob later. And she could meet the rest of Bob's family *much* later. Like at the rehearsal dinner. Even Mom realized that all those people might be a little much for T. J.'s first couple of nights here.

My mom had made up the couch in the den for T. J. We decided we'd ask her if she wanted a room at our new house. It would be totally up to her. We all knew she wasn't going to live with us, but she was welcome to visit anytime. For as long as she wanted.

"Are you nervous?" Mom asked as we drove into Cedar Rapids.

"Yes," I said. "Are you?"

"Yes." Mom smiled.

We parked a couple of blocks away from the bus station, then walked back. It was a nice day, so we decided to wait outside.

I checked my watch. Ten minutes. T. J. would be here in ten minutes.

"Do you think she's nervous?" I asked.

"I'm sure she's terrified," Mom answered. "This is a big step for her, coming for the wedding. It's a big step for all of us."

T. J. wasn't going to be *in* the wedding like me, she was just coming *for* the wedding. She would be here for one week. And maybe, just maybe, I would go there, to Joe and T. J.'s house for a long weekend in October when we were off from school. Mom was still thinking about that.

"Look! I think this is her bus!" I said as a big bus came around the corner and slowly pulled into the parking lot.

As the door to the bus wheezed open, Mom and I grabbed hands. Her hand was just as sweaty as mine.

We watched anxiously as all the people filed off the bus. A woman my mom's age with a little kid, two guys in jeans and T-shirts, an older lady with a flowery dress, and finally...T. J.

She smiled a little when she saw us. She hoisted a medium-sized duffel bag onto her shoulder and walked over to us.

"Hey," she said, stopping in front of me.

"Hey," I said back.

It wasn't much, but it was a start.

Dori Hillestad Butler is the author of many works of fiction and nonfiction for young readers. Her middle grade novel *Sliding into Home* has received numerous awards, including an Honor Book Award from the Society of School Librarians International. She has also been nominated for children's choice awards in nineteen different states. Dori lives in Washington.

Visit her website at *www.kidswriter.com.*